The Avion Menace

Navy Seal Turned into Spy,

Ceased the Threat from the Sky.

Pranav Jariwala

This book is a work of fiction and, except in the case of historical fact any resemblance to actual persons, living or dead, is purely coincidental.

ISBN: 978-93-5408-748-6

Publisher: Self Publish.

Contents

Chapter 1: The Murder.

The morning sun, a vibrant kiss on Manhattan, painted Dr. Victor Spectre's duplex penthouse in a warm, golden hue. Yet, a sense of urgency, a familiar pre-work jitters, stirred within him. He glanced at his reflection, the mirror reflecting a man caught in the whirlwind of a busy New York life.

The rhythmic tap of his footsteps on the wooden stairs echoed through the quiet apartment, drawing him closer to the kitchen. The air was thick with the enticing aroma of breakfast – Veronica's specialty. His wife, a whirlwind of grace and efficiency, moved with the practiced ease of a seasoned chef. Their eyes met, a silent acknowledgment of their shared morning ritual.

"Good morning, Vic," Veronica greeted him, her voice warm and welcoming. "Pancakes are ready, just the way you like them."

Their love story, a classic New York romance, had blossomed at a friend's party. It was love at first sight, a connection that transcended the city's frenetic energy. Twenty years later, their bond remained as strong as ever, a testament to their unwavering support and enduring love.

Veronica, a distinguished professor of economics at NYU, was a force to be reckoned with. Her sharp intellect and unwavering support had been instrumental in Victor's success.

"Where's Roy?" Victor inquired, his gaze sweeping the kitchen. "Shouldn't he be off to school?"

"Roy!" Veronica's voice echoed through the apartment. "Hurry up, breakfast is getting cold!"

Their son, Roy, a twelve-year-old whirlwind of energy and intelligence, was a carbon copy of his father. Their bond, a unique blend of friendship and father-son love, was a source of immense pride for Victor.

Roy, humming a catchy tune, emerged from his bathroom, his face still damp from his shower.

"Morning, Mom, morning, Dad," he greeted them, his voice brimming with youthful enthusiasm.

He joined them at the table, eager to devour the pancakes.

"Dad," Roy announced, "Can you come to my school tomorrow morning? Mom has a meeting, so I thought you could go in her place."

"Of course, son," Victor assured him. "No problem at all."

Breakfast was a lively affair, filled with the cheerful chatter of father and son. Soon, it was time for Roy to head off to school.

Victor, a man who cherished the finer things in life, especially his prized possession – a sleek, black Mercedes-Benz S63 AMG – navigated the morning traffic with a practiced ease. Manhattan, a concrete jungle teeming with ambition, presented its daily challenge – the relentless crawl of traffic.

Finally, he arrived at his office, the gleaming headquarters of Victory defence Systems, a company he had co-founded with his college friend, Brian McQueen. Their partnership, forged in the crucible of MIT, had blossomed into a formidable force in the world of weapons technology.

Brian, the charismatic salesman, handled the business end, while Victor, the visionary, spearheaded the cutting-edge research and development. Their complementary strengths had propelled Victory Defence Systems to the forefront of the industry.

However, beneath the veneer of success, a subtle undercurrent of tension had begun to simmer. Brian, driven by an insatiable greed, had started to entertain the unthinkable – selling their advanced weaponry to the highest bidder, regardless of the ethical implications.

Victor, in his secluded lab, poured over the blueprints of his latest creation – an Electromagnetic Pulse device, or EMP, for short. This revolutionary technology, capable of disabling electronic systems over a vast area, was both a marvel of engineering and a potential weapon of immense destruction.

Brian, unable to resist the lure of easy profits, approached Victor with his proposition.

"We could make a fortune, Vic," Brian argued, his eyes gleaming with avarice. "Selling these weapons to the highest bidder, regardless of who they are."

Victor recoiled, his voice firm. "Are you out of your mind? We're not mercenaries, Brian. Our integrity is more important than any amount of money."

Brian, frustrated by Victor's unwavering moral compass, dismissed his concerns. "Get real, Vic. This is business. We maximize profits, that's the bottom line."

Victor remained adamant, refusing to compromise his principles. However, Brian, fueled by greed and a simmering resentment towards Victor's superior intellect, continued to explore illicit avenues.

Victor, sensing the danger, began to discreetly monitor Brian's activities. He knew he had to be vigilant, to protect his creation from falling into the wrong hands.

The following day, Victor and Brian were scheduled to present their EMP device to Paul Wright, the head of the Department of Defense. The anticipation was palpable.

As Victor meticulously fine-tuned the device, a sense of foreboding crept into his mind. The power of this technology, he realized, was a double-edged sword. In the wrong hands, it could wreak havoc, plunging the world into chaos.

To mitigate this risk, Victor devised a failsafe – a crucial circuit that was essential for the device's activation. He removed the circuit and, in a moment of inspiration, decided to hide it in an unexpected place – the head of Roy's new toy robot.

Later that evening, Victor presented Roy with the coveted robot, watching his son's eyes light up with excitement.

"Thank you, Dad!" Roy exclaimed, his voice filled with gratitude. "This is the coolest thing ever!"

Victor smiled, a pang of bittersweet emotion stirring within him. He had hidden the circuit within the robot, a seemingly innocuous object, hoping to keep it safe from prying eyes.

However, his carefully laid plans were soon shattered. In the dead of night, a chilling alarm shattered the peace of their home.

"Veronica!" Victor cried, his heart pounding. "It's the lab! Someone's trying to steal the device!"

He rushed out of the house, his mind racing. As he approached the lab, a horrifying scene unfolded before his eyes. The security guard lay unconscious, the door to the research facility wide open.

Inside, a masked figure stood over the EMP device, their movements swift and determined.

"Stop!" Victor roared, lunging towards the intruder.

A vicious struggle ensued. The intruder, armed with a screwdriver, fought back with brutal ferocity.

Victor, despite his valiant efforts, was no match for his attacker. The sharp metal pierced his flesh, again and again.

As the life drained from his body, Victor's mind flashed with images of his beloved wife, his cherished son, their shared laughter, their dreams for the future.

The intruder, panicked, snatched the device and vanished into the night, leaving behind a trail of blood and a shattered silence.

The next morning, Alisha, Victor's assistant, arrived at the office, unaware of the tragedy that had unfolded. As she entered the research lab, a bloodcurdling scream escaped her lips.

Victor lay lifeless on the floor, his body riddled with wounds. The EMP device, his masterpiece, was gone.

The news of Victor's murder sent shockwaves through the company. Brian, outwardly grief-stricken, concealed a flicker of satisfaction behind his facade of mourning.

Detective George Gregor, a seasoned NYPD detective, arrived at the scene, his gaze fixed on the gruesome spectacle.

"Murder," he declared, his voice grave. "But why? And who would want to kill Dr. Spectre?"

Veronica, her face pale and drawn, arrived at the scene, her heart heavy with grief.

"I don't understand," she whispered, her voice trembling. "Victor had no enemies. He was kind, compassionate, always willing to help others."

Detective Gregor, his eyes narrowed, began his investigation. The mystery deepened with each passing hour. Was it a robbery gone wrong? Or was something more sinister at play?

The death of Dr. Victor Spectre, a brilliant scientist, a loving husband, and a devoted father, cast a long shadow over the city that never sleeps. And as the investigation unfolded, it became clear that the repercussions of his murder would reverberate far beyond the confines of his laboratory

Chapter 2: The NYPD Detective.

Detective George Gregor, a name synonymous with justice in New York City, stood as a testament to bravery and intellect. His chest bore the weight of honor – the "Medal of Honor," the "Medal for Valour," and the coveted "Police Combat Cross." Within the NYPD, his team boasted the highest case closure rate, a reflection of Gregor's uncanny ability to extract confessions. His methods, sometimes bordering on aggressive, were a point of contention among his colleagues, yet his results were undeniable. He possessed a keen understanding of the criminal psyche, knowing precisely which pressure points to exploit.

The case that earned him the Medal of Honor remained a vivid memory. A year prior, a chilling call had summoned him to Central Park.

"George, homicide at Central Park," the voice on the other end of the line crackled at approximately 7:00 AM. "Call came in about fifteen minutes ago."

"Understood. I'll be there shortly," Gregor replied, still groggy from sleep. He hastily brewed a cup of coffee, poured it into a travel mug, and sped towards the crime scene.

The sight that greeted him was grim – a man sprawled on his back, a crimson stain blooming across his chest. The Medical Examiner was already on site, his expression somber.

"Male, approximately five-eleven," the M.E. stated, his voice clinical. "Three gunshot wounds to the chest. Estimated time of death between midnight and two AM."

"Who reported the body?" Gregor inquired, his eyes scanning the surroundings.

"A jogger named Jerry," Detective Tom answered. "Found him around six forty-five this morning."

"Any identification on the victim?"

"Yes," the M.E. replied. "Austin Assange. Works at the Mayor's Office. His ID identifies him as the Mayor's assistant."

Gregor knelt beside the body, his gaze sharp. "What's that stain on his shirt?"

Tom leaned in, sniffing cautiously. "Looks like a coffee stain, Boss."

"Canvass the nearby cafeterias," Gregor instructed. "Show them Assange's photograph. If anyone has any information, have them call me immediately."

Tom embarked on his task, locating three cafeterias within the vicinity. The first two yielded nothing, but at the third, the owner's eyes widened in recognition.

"Yeah, I remember him," the owner said. "He was wearing a hoodie, looked all stressed out. Ordered a coffee, and then my waitress, bless her heart, spilled it all over him. He just about jumped out of his skin and stormed off."

"Any chance I could see the CCTV footage from that time?" Tom asked.

"Sure thing," the owner agreed.

The grainy footage revealed Austin Assange sitting alone, his posture tense. He appeared to be surreptitiously observing two men at a nearby table, his gaze darting nervously. It looked as though he was straining to overhear their conversation.

Tom secured the footage and hurried back to the precinct to show it to Gregor.

"Recognize the man Assange was eavesdropping on?" Gregor asked, his eyes glued to the screen.

"No sir, nothing familiar," Tom replied.

"What about the other man at the table? The one with his back to the camera. Looks like he's deliberately avoiding being seen."

"You're right, Boss."

"Alright," Gregor decided. "I'm heading to the Mayor's Office. I need to speak with him about Assange."

The Mayor's Office buzzed with activity. Gregor rode the elevator to the top floor, observing the purposeful stride of the staff. He approached the receptionist.

"Good afternoon," Gregor announced, flashing his badge. "Detective George Gregor, NYPD. I need to see the Mayor."

"Please wait a moment, Detective. He'll be with you shortly."

A few minutes later, Gregor was ushered into the Mayor's spacious office.

"Good afternoon, Mayor," Gregor began. "I'm here to investigate the murder of your assistant, Austin."

"George, good to see you," the Mayor replied, extending a hand. "It's been too long."

"Likewise, Mr. Mayor. I have some questions regarding Assange."

"Poor fellow," the Mayor sighed. "A bright young man. I'm devastated. Please, find whoever did this. You have my full cooperation."

"Thank you, Mayor. Could you tell me what time Austin left the office yesterday?"

"He mentioned meeting his girlfriend and requested leave around three PM. That was the last I saw of him."

"Did he have any known enemies? Or had you noticed any changes in his behaviour recently?"

"Not that I'm aware of. You should probably speak with his girlfriend, Jennifer. She might have more insight than I do."

"Understood. Thank you for your time, Mayor."

"My pleasure, George. Don't hesitate to reach out if you need anything."

"Will do, Mayor," Gregor replied.

Gregor then made his way to Jennifer's apartment, a weathered five-story building. Opting for the stairs due to the out-of-service elevator, he climbed to the third floor and found the corner apartment. He knocked.

Jennifer opened the door, her eyes red and swollen.

"Hello, Jennifer. Detective George Gregor, NYPD. I have some questions about Austin."

"Please," she choked out, stepping aside. "Come in."

Gregor entered the small apartment. "When was the last time you saw Austin?"

"We were together for about a year," Jennifer began, her voice thick with emotion. "He was so kind, so loyal. Yesterday, he asked me to meet him in Central Park around four. We spent some time there, and then around seven, we went to a nearby bar for drinks and dinner. We left around eleven. As we were leaving, he saw something that made him really nervous. When I asked him what was wrong, he just said everything was fine. Then he told me to take a cab because he had some unfinished work to do."

"Did you notice anything unusual about his behaviour?"

"No, everything seemed normal, except for that moment when he saw someone as we were leaving. He just… he seemed really troubled. And then he insisted I take a cab."

"Alright. Thank you for your time, Jennifer," Gregor said, his mind already piecing together the fragments. He felt like he was back at square one.

Suddenly, he remembered the photographs of the mysterious man. He hadn't shown them to the Mayor. He returned to the Mayor's Office.

"Mr. Mayor," Gregor asked, presenting the images. "Do you recognize this man sitting with Austin's tablemate?"

"Yes," the Mayor replied without hesitation. "That's Justin, my head of security."

"Austin was last seen at the cafeteria, apparently overhearing Justin talking to someone. I suspect he heard something he shouldn't have, and that's why he was killed. Where can I find Justin?"

"I'm not sure where he is right now. He hasn't come in for duty today. My staff can provide you with his contact information."

"Thank you again," Gregor said.

Gregor obtained Justin's address and called Tom, instructing him to apprehend Justin and bring him to the precinct. But when Tom arrived at Justin's residence, the apartment was empty. His phone was also off. Tom relayed the information to Gregor.

"Justin's not at his place, Boss. And his phone's dead."

"Alright," Gregor sighed. "We need to issue a BOLO on Justin immediately."

The following day, Justin was apprehended at a friend's house. Gregor entered the interrogation room, his gaze unwavering.

"Justin," Gregor began, his voice firm. "You were a hard man to find. Now, tell me about Austin Assange. How did you kill him?"

"I didn't kill him! I don't know what you're talking about."

"Cooperate with us, confess, and we'll recommend the DA reduce your sentence. Refuse, and you'll face the full consequences."

"I told you, I don't know anything about Assange."

"Don't play games with us, Justin. We have the footage from the cafeteria. You were sitting with someone, and Assange was right next to you. His death occurred shortly after you left. You realized who he was, followed him, and silenced him."

"Okay, okay," Justin relented, his bravado crumbling. "I'll tell you everything, but I need protection. If I talk, my life won't be worth anything, even in jail."

"Tell me what happened," Gregor pressed.

"A businessman, Max Edinburgh, hired me to kill the Mayor. He's furious because the Mayor shut down his construction site. Edinburgh's already invested millions, and the Mayor won't give him the permits. He told me to make it look like a suicide. He paid me fifty thousand dollars. Assange overheard everything, so Edinburgh told me to kill him too, to keep his plan secret."

Gregor had Justin remanded to custody. Tom confirmed the fifty-thousand-dollar transfer in Justin's bank account. Gregor immediately ordered the arrest of Max Edinburgh. However, when the officers arrived at his Manhattan penthouse, Edinburgh was gone. He had vanished.

Gregor rushed to the Mayor's Office to inform him of the developments and warn him of the imminent danger.

"Mr. Mayor," Gregor said urgently. "Your life is in danger. Max Edinburgh hired your own head of security, Justin, to kill you and stage it as a suicide. I'm assigning two of my best officers to your protection immediately."

"Thank you, George," the Mayor said, his face grim. "Edinburgh has been pressuring me relentlessly to approve his project. He's tried everything. I suppose this was his last resort."

"Don't worry, Mr. Mayor. We've issued a BOLO on Edinburgh. He'll be apprehended soon. But we need to be vigilant."

As night fell, Gregor and the Mayor left the office. They descended the stairs and headed towards their cars. As they approached the curb, Gregor's eyes caught a figure across the street. The man pulled a gun from his jacket, aiming it directly at the Mayor. In a split-second decision, Gregor lunged forward, shielding the Mayor. A bullet ripped through his hand. The other two officers reacted instantly, firing at the assailant, killing him on the spot. It was Max Edinburgh.

Gregor was rushed to the hospital. The Mayor, deeply grateful for Gregor's bravery and quick thinking, visited him and personally awarded him a second "Medal of Honor."

Victor's murder investigation weighed heavily on Gregor. Despite his meticulous efforts, he found no concrete evidence leading to the killer and the thief. The CCTV footage from that day had been completely erased. The perpetrator had left no discernible trace. Eventually, the NYPD closed the case, unsolved.

One morning, Veronica left for the university earlier than usual. En route, she realized she had forgotten her cell phone. Returning home, she noticed the front door lock was broken. A knot of fear tightened in her stomach. She entered cautiously, her senses on high alert. The living room was in disarray, furniture overturned, belongings scattered. She rushed to her bedroom, then to Roy's, but nothing of obvious value appeared to be missing. She immediately called the NYPD.

The police conducted a thorough search, but the scene offered little in the way of clues. The detective on the case suggested to Veronica that the intruder might have been searching for something specific, something not immediately apparent. He asked if she knew of any valuable possessions of Victor's that someone might be interested in. Veronica, bewildered, could offer no explanation.

Roy returned from school to the shocking sight of his ransacked home. He hugged his mother, his young face etched with worry. He went to his room, his toys strewn across the floor. He began searching for his beloved robot. He found it tucked away in a corner, and relief washed over him as he picked it up. As he grasped its head, it accidentally detached, and the robot fell to the floor. A small, unfamiliar circuit board tumbled out. Unaware of its significance, Roy simply placed it back inside, reattached the robot's head, and resumed playing.

A month passed, and a semblance of normalcy returned to Veronica and Roy's lives. Veronica sat in the living room, watching television. Roy joined her on the couch.

"It's been a month since Dad died," Roy said quietly. "Sometimes, I still feel like he's here."

Tears welled in Veronica's eyes. "I know, sweetheart. It's hard for both of us. But your father wouldn't want us to be consumed by grief. We have to be strong, for him."

"Mom," Roy declared, his voice filled with a newfound resolve, "I swear, whoever did this to Dad, I'm going to find them. I'll make them pay."

The news channel on television suddenly flashed a breaking story: Brian McQueen, Victor's partner at Victory Defence Systems, had been killed in a boating accident during a rafting trip. Authorities were searching for his body.

Veronica and Roy exchanged shocked glances.

"Mom, look! Uncle Brian… dead?" Roy stammered.

"This is unbelievable," Veronica whispered. "First Victor, and now Brian…"

"Mom, this doesn't feel right," Roy said, a flicker of suspicion in his young eyes.

"No, it doesn't, Roy. I don't know what's happening."

They both felt a prickle of unease, a sense of something dark lurking beneath the surface, but eventually, they pushed the unsettling thoughts aside. Days turned into weeks, and Brian's body was never recovered.

In the aftermath of Victor's death, a subtle shift occurred in Roy. A quiet intensity settled within him. The desire for justice for his father seemed to sharpen his senses. He became acutely observant, noticing nuances in human behavior, studying tells and inconsistencies. He immersed himself in online puzzles and mysteries, honing his analytical skills. He paid attention to details – clothing, stains, subtle gestures, scars. This newfound awareness transformed him. He became surprisingly adept at reading people, a silent observer who often knew more than he let on.

Chapter 3: The University Life.

Years spun by, and Roy traded the familiar halls of his school for the sprawling campus of Columbia University. University life unfolded as a vibrant tapestry of experiences, unburdened by financial constraints, thanks to the considerable inheritance left by his father, Victor. Roy embraced it all with an almost reckless abandon. The roar of his sports car, the subtle sheen of branded clothes, and the pulsating rhythm of his parties became his calling cards. He was a figure of considerable notoriety on campus, his striking looks, honed physique, and undeniable wealth attracting a constant orbit of admirers. Each night seemed to introduce him to a new, captivating woman, each drawn to his magnetic presence.

One day, a disquieting discovery disrupted the easy rhythm of Roy's life. His closest friend, Rick, who resided in the university hostel, had been the victim of a theft. His laptop, cell phone, and a cherished diamond ring, a legacy from his grandfather, were gone. Roy, whose mind naturally gravitated towards puzzles and mysteries, visited Rick's ransacked room, a scene of jarring disarray.

"Rick, look at this place," Roy exclaimed, his gaze sweeping over the overturned furniture and scattered belongings. "The thief really turned it upside down."

"Yeah, man," Rick replied, his voice tight with anxiety. "But my laptop, my phone… and this ring," he gestured to his bare finger. "My grandfather gave it to me. Roy, you have to do something. Help me find my things. I have sensitive data on my phone and laptop."

"Don't worry, bro," Roy assured him, a spark of intrigue in his eyes. "You'll have your belongings back by the end of the day."

"What? By the end of the day? How? Do you know who stole them?"

"Not definitively, not yet. But give me some time. Don't touch anything. Let me investigate. I'm sure the burglar left some kind of evidence."

"Okay," Rick said, a hint of skepticism in his voice. "So, suddenly you're Sherlock Holmes."

"Do you want your stuff back or not?"

"Yeah, I do."

"Then trust me," Roy said with a confident nod.

Roy began a meticulous examination of the room, his eyes scanning every inch for a telltale sign. In a dusty corner, he spotted a small, broken piece of a keychain snagged on the carpet. He picked it up, turning it over in his fingers. Suddenly, a vivid image flashed through his mind, a fleeting glimpse from his memory.

"You know our classmate Mathew, right?" Roy asked Rick.

"Yeah, why?"

"Look at this broken keychain part. Where have you seen this before?"

Rick frowned, his brow furrowed in concentration. "Wait a minute… Mathew had a keychain just like that! I remember seeing it on his car keys. Yeah! Now it's coming back to me. A couple of days ago, we had a really bad argument about Marissa. She likes me, and Mathew's also got a thing for her. He threatened me, said he'd ruin my life. I bet he's behind this. He'll probably leak some of my private photos and videos online to trash my reputation."

"Yeah, you're probably right," Roy agreed grimly.

"We have to do something fast! If those videos and photos get out, my life will be over!"

"Don't worry," Roy said, his voice firm. "Let's go to his room and confront him about the theft. And hey, you don't say a word. Let me do the talking."

Roy's keen observational skills, honed by a subconscious desire to understand the darkness that had claimed his father, were beginning to pay dividends. He and Rick walked to Mathew's dorm room and knocked. Mathew opened the door, a look of feigned innocence on his face.

"What's up, Mathew?" Roy asked casually. "I was just admiring your car keychain the other day. I was thinking of getting one like it."

Unaware that Roy had found the broken piece, Mathew confidently reached into his pocket and produced his car keys.

"See? This one?" he said, holding them up.

A look of confusion flickered across Mathew's face as he realized the keychain was missing. While Mathew patted his pockets with increasing desperation, Roy calmly held out the broken piece he had found in Rick's room.

"Not finding your keychain, Mathew? Wait! Here it is. Looks like you forgot it in Rick's room."

Mathew's composure crumbled. Before he could formulate a lie, Roy pushed past him and strode into the room. His eyes immediately landed on Rick's laptop, cell phone, and diamond ring, lying conspicuously on the desk.

"What is this, Mathew?" Roy's voice was sharp. "How did Rick's things end up in your room?"

"I… I… I don't know anything about it," Mathew stammered, his face pale.

"So, they sprouted legs and walked in here on their own, did they?"

"Seriously, guys, I have no idea."

"Drop the act, Mathew," Roy said, his gaze unwavering. "You're busted."

Rick retrieved his belongings, his relief palpable. Roy turned to Mathew, his expression a warning.

"If you ever try pulling something like this again on Rick or anyone else, you'll regret it deeply."

A year at Columbia had passed in a blur of academic pursuits and social engagements. Roy had recently returned from a lavish European vacation with his mother, the lingering languor of the holiday making the prospect of returning to classes unappealing. It was a glorious, sun-drenched day, and he chose to spend it relaxing on campus with his friends. The air hummed with the murmur of conversations, punctuated by bursts of laughter and playful banter. Couples strolled hand-in-hand, some lost in private worlds, others engaged in hushed disputes – the vibrant tapestry of university life unfolding around them.

Roy sat in the dappled shade of the campus garden, sharing a joke with a friend, when his eyes were suddenly arrested by the sight of a girl entering the university grounds. His breath hitched, his heart stuttering at the sheer beauty of her. Blonde hair cascaded around her shoulders like spun gold, framing eyes the color of a summer sky. Her figure was graceful, her presence so captivating that Roy felt an immediate, almost cinematic, connection. It was, undeniably, love at first sight, a moment so cliché it felt almost surreal.

"Wow," he thought, utterly mesmerized. "I've never seen anyone so beautiful."

Noticing his friend's sudden, almost comical, state of stupefaction, Rick playfully nudged him.

"Earth to Roy! I've been trying to get your attention for ages. What planet are you on?"

"Huh? Oh, yeah! You wait here. I'll be right back," Roy mumbled, his gaze still fixed on the girl as she moved through the crowd.

He rose abruptly and hurried after her, but by the time he reached the bustling walkway, she had vanished. A wave of unexpected disappointment washed over him.

The following day, as Roy walked down a busy corridor, he saw her again – the ethereal girl from the previous afternoon. A jolt of excitement shot through him, and he instinctively quickened his pace. It appeared to be her first day; she seemed slightly disoriented, her gaze sweeping over the unfamiliar surroundings.

"She looks a little lost," Roy thought, a surge of chivalry rising within him. "Maybe I can help."

A nervous flutter danced in his stomach as he approached her.

"Hello," he began, trying to project an air of casual confidence. "Can I help you with something?"

"Oh, yes! Please. I'm trying to find my class. Would you mind pointing me in the right direction?"

"Absolutely. Walk with me. I'll escort you to your classroom."

As they strolled together, Roy's heart hammered against his ribs, a rush of adrenaline and anticipation coursing through him. The classroom appeared sooner than he expected. He gestured towards the door with a warm smile. The girl offered a grateful look.

"Thank you so much," she said, turning to enter the room.

"By the way," Roy called out, a touch of nervousness lacing his voice, "my name is Roy Spectre."

"Hi, Roy. I'm Christina Muller. And thank you again for your help."

"Oh, it's my pleasure, Christina. You are… breathtakingly beautiful."

"Thanks, Roy," Christina replied, a delicate blush blooming on her cheeks.

A wave of simultaneous nervousness and elation washed over Roy. Their eyes met for a fleeting moment, a silent acknowledgment of the burgeoning attraction, before they turned and went their separate ways.

A few days later, a raucous party filled the air with thumping music and the clinking of glasses. Roy and Rick joined the throng. The scene was a sensory overload – flashing lights, the potent aroma of alcohol, and a sea of beautiful faces in various states of intoxication. As the night deepened and inhibitions dissolved, the party devolved into the predictable chaos of college revelry. Suddenly, a figure in the doorway caught Roy's eye, and his breath hitched. It was Christina. His elusive crush was here. He navigated the crowded room towards her.

"Hey, Christina! What's up? Are you enjoying the party?"

"Hey Roy! I'm good. It's… lively," she replied with a wry smile.

"Well, it's about to get a whole lot more interesting," Roy said, a playful glint in his eyes.

"Oh, really?" she teased, a hint of color rising in her cheeks.

"Can I get you a drink?"

"Sure."

Roy returned with a vodka for Christina, and they retreated to a slightly quieter corner of the room. The music was still loud enough to necessitate raised voices.

"This is a bit intense," Christina said, gesturing towards the gyrating bodies. "Is there somewhere a little less… deafening we could talk?"

"Yeah, there's a garden out back. Let's go there."

They found a secluded bench nestled amongst the greenery. A comfortable silence settled between them, the unspoken attraction hanging heavy in the night air.

"You know," Roy began, his gaze intent on her, "you are the most beautiful woman I have ever seen. I honestly can't take my eyes off you."

"You know," Christina replied softly, her eyes mirroring his intensity, "I like you too, Roy. You're kind and helpful. You're quite different from what I initially thought, but after getting to know you, I've really started to like you."

"What was your first impression?" Roy asked, a genuine curiosity in his voice.

"At first," she admitted, a playful smile gracing her lips, "you seemed a little… spoiled. But you're much more than that."

Christina's own nervousness mirrored Roy's. He gently reached out, his hand cupping her cheek, his eyes locked on hers. Their hearts pounded in unison. A palpable tension filled the space between them. Roy leaned closer, their gazes unwavering, until his lips finally brushed against hers. A soft, tentative kiss that quickly deepened into something more profound. They embraced, a tight, heartfelt hug.

"Christina," Roy whispered, his voice thick with emotion, "I love you."

"I love you too, Roy," she replied, her voice equally tender.

Spring unfolded its delicate beauty across the campus. Flowers burst into vibrant color, new leaves unfurled on the trees, and the days stretched into golden evenings. Roy and Christina walked hand-in-hand through the park, Christina's head resting comfortably on Roy's shoulder. They settled on a secluded bench beneath the crimson canopy of a red maple tree, the world around them bathed in a soft, romantic light. Roy gazed into Christina's eyes, a profound sense of contentment washing over him.

"Roy," Christina asked softly, breaking the comfortable silence, "tell me something about your family."

"It's just my mom now," Roy replied, a fleeting shadow crossing his features. "My father was murdered a few years ago."

"Oh, Roy, I'm so sorry for your loss," Christina said, her hand tightening around his. "Do you mind if I ask what happened? Who… who murdered him?"

"My father was a weapon inventor," Roy explained, his voice tinged with a lingering sadness. "I don't know who killed him. He was working on some kind of dangerous weapon. I think that's why he was targeted."

"What kind of weapon?"

"I think it was some sort of EMP device. He finally finished it after years of hard work. Whoever killed him also took it."

Sensing the shift in Roy's mood, the familiar pain resurfacing, Christina gently took his hand, her touch a silent reassurance.

"So," she said, her voice regaining its playful lilt, "it's the weekend. Any plans for tonight? Because if you don't, I might have some rather… naughty plans for us."

Roy's eyebrows shot up, a slow smile spreading across his face.

"Hmm, naughty plans, you say? I do like naughty plans."

He pulled Christina closer, about to kiss her, but she placed a teasing finger on his lips.

"Wait, baby. Wait until tonight."

"Alright, alright," Roy chuckled, his anticipation building. "Let's hurry up then. Let me finish up some things, and I'll see you this evening."

Roy rushed home, a thrill of excitement coursing through him. He indulged in a long, warm bath and meticulously prepared for Christina's arrival. He carefully styled his hair, chose a crisp white shirt that accentuated his physique, and added a subtle touch of his favourite cologne. The evening stretched before him, brimming with promise.

The doorbell chimed, and Roy practically sprinted to the door. He swung it open, his breath catching in his throat. Christina stood before him, an absolute vision in a delicate red tube gown that clung to her curves like a second skin. Her lips were painted a seductive red, her eyes smouldered with a smoky allure. She was utterly enchanting.

"Oh, wow," Roy breathed, stepping aside to welcome her in. "You look absolutely stunning, my lady. Hot."

"Thank you," Christina purred, her eyes twinkling. "You clean up nicely yourself."

"Come in quickly. I have a little surprise for you too."

Roy had transformed his apartment into a haven of romance. A beautifully set table glowed under the soft light of flickering candles. He had even ordered Christina's favorite dishes from her beloved restaurant. Taking her hand, he led her to the table and gallantly seated her.

"Nice," Christina said, her eyes sweeping over the intimate setting. "I'm impressed, Roy. Very well arranged."

"My pleasure, my lady," Roy replied with a charming smile.

He poured two glasses of chilled champagne, and they raised a toast.

"To a beautiful night," Roy said, his gaze locking with hers, "and to many more."

After a leisurely and romantic dinner, Roy cued up Christina's favourite song. He extended his hand.

"My lady, would you care to dance with me?"

"I would," she replied, her smile radiant.

They swayed together, Roy's hand resting gently on the small of Christina's back, drawing her close. The atmosphere was charged with a tender intimacy, the soothing melody weaving a spell around them. Lost in each other's eyes, the warm candlelight casting soft shadows, the world outside ceased to exist.

Slowly, passionately, Roy leaned forward, his gaze drawn to Christina's luscious lips. They kissed, a deep, lingering kiss that spoke volumes of their burgeoning love and desire. A mutual urgency took hold. While their lips were still entwined, Roy gently began to ease the delicate fabric of Christina's gown from her shoulders, and she, in turn, eagerly unbuttoned his shirt. The air crackled with anticipation. Christina playfully pushed Roy towards the plush couch. In the ensuing moments, two souls intertwined, seeking the profound connection of shared intimacy. They reached the crescendo of their passion, and with a shared sigh of satisfaction, they held each other close, soft kisses and tender touches sealing the memory of a night etched in the annals of their burgeoning love story.

Chapter 4: Holiday.

The weekend stretched before Roy, an expanse of unscheduled time. Christina was away, visiting her grandmother in Philadelphia, leaving a quiet void in his usually vibrant life. He leaned against the plush cushions of his couch, the television screen flickering with uninspired images, a mirror to his own listless mood. A sense of restless energy began to stir within him.

"Why not?" he mused aloud. "I'll give Rick a call. He's probably free, it being the weekend and all."

His fingers danced across his phone screen, dialling Rick's number.

"Hey, mate, what's up?" Rick's cheerful voice boomed through the receiver.

"Rick, are you free today?"

"Yeah! What's the plan?"

"Nothing much, bro. Just feeling a bit bored, all alone here. I was thinking, shall we head down to my vacation home in Maryland? It's about a three-and-a-half-hour drive. It's ten AM now; if we leave by ten-thirty, we could be there around one-thirty. How about we stay the night?"

"Yeah, man, that sounds awesome. Let's do it."

Roy pushed himself off the couch, a sudden surge of enthusiasm replacing his boredom. He grabbed a backpack from his room and tossed in a few changes of clothes. Snatching his car keys from the hook beside the door, he headed out to pick up Rick. On the way, he dialed Christina's number.

"Hey, babe! Rick and I are heading down to our vacation home in Maryland for the night. We were both getting a bit stir-crazy and thought a weekend at the beach house would do us good."

Christina's voice, tinged with a touch of wistfulness, came through the phone. "Oh, that sounds lovely. I'm getting a bit bored at Grandma's too. I wish I could be there with you. Remember that time we went together? That was so much fun. Anyway, you guys have a great time."

Roy arrived at Rick's place, the powerful engine of his Camaro rumbling to a stop. He leaned on the horn.

"Rick, where are you?"

"Two minutes, mate, coming!" Rick yelled back.

Moments later, Rick burst out of the house, a duffel bag slung over his shoulder and a case of beer clutched in his hand.

"Roy, pop the trunk!"

Roy pressed the button, and the trunk sprang open. Rick tossed in his bag and carefully placed the case of beer inside. He then hopped into the passenger seat, slapping a high-five with Roy as the latter engaged the first gear. Their journey to Maryland began, the car filled with the thumping bass and soaring vocals of The Weeknd's "Blinding Lights," Roy nodding his head in time with the rhythm, mouthing the lyrics with gusto. The open highway stretched before them, promising a welcome escape, the adrenaline and excitement building with each passing mile as they drew closer to their beachside retreat.

"Rick," Roy said over the music, "it's been way too long since we've just taken off like this. This is going to be a blast, mate."

"Yeah, bro," Rick agreed, grinning. "A proper weekend getaway."

"You know, Rick," Roy continued, "your spur-of-the-moment ideas are always the best. I can already picture it – chilling at the beach house, a cold beer in hand, watching the sunset."

"Man, you're making me even more hyped up! Floor it, let's get to Maryland pronto!" Rick urged.

Roy obliged, pressing down on the accelerator. The Camaro responded with a satisfying surge of power. Twenty miles remained until their destination. A notification popped up on the map displayed on Roy's phone: "ETA: 45 minutes."

"Forty-five minutes to pure relaxation, bro," Roy announced.

"Yo! Just forty-five minutes!" Rick echoed.

They crossed the Maryland state line.

"Welcome to Maryland," Roy declared.

They navigated towards "Thomas Point Road," and within minutes, familiar landmarks began to appear.

"Where is house number 4200?" Roy muttered, peering through the windshield at the succession of bungalows lining the road. Finally, he spotted the number. "There it is! Turn left."

"At last," Rick sighed contentedly as Roy pulled into the driveway. "We've arrived, brother."

"Damn, man," Rick exclaimed, his eyes wide as he took in the sprawling property. "Your house is huge and looks seriously luxurious. I love it."

"That's just the outside, Rick," Roy said with a grin. "Wait till you see the inside and the view from the house. You'll be blown away."

They both climbed out of the car. Roy popped the trunk, and they retrieved their bags and the case of beer. Roy locked the car, and they headed towards the house. He unlocked the front door, and they stepped inside. Rick, a first-time visitor, wandered through the house with a look of fascinated curiosity. Roy dropped their bags on a plush couch and made his way to the spacious kitchen to stash the beer in the refrigerator.

"Man, your house is truly incredible," Rick said, his gaze sweeping over the elegant furnishings. "Your dad had impeccable taste, I must say."

"Yeah, Rick," Roy agreed, a touch of pride in his voice. "He really did. He personally oversaw the entire interior design, paying attention to every single detail during construction."

The house exuded the charm of a French villa, seamlessly blending with a relaxed beach house vibe. A grand, double-height living room boasted a magnificent chandelier, its light reflecting off the bright, airy walls. Comfortable couches invited relaxation. The kitchen was a culinary dream, featuring sleek white stone countertops. Amenities like a table tennis setup, a pool table, and a state-of-the-art video game console hinted at leisure and entertainment. Large, elegant curtains framed expansive windows that offered breath-taking views of the shimmering green ocean and the pristine white sand of the beach. The fresh, salty aroma of the sea filled the air, creating an atmosphere of tranquillity and escape.

Roy gave Rick a comprehensive tour of the house, culminating in the backyard, where a large pool overlooked the mesmerizing ocean. The gentle rhythm of the waves provided a soothing soundtrack, washing away any lingering stress.

"Roy," Rick said, his voice hushed with awe, "the view is absolutely spectacular. Just looking at it makes me feel instantly relaxed."

"Tell me about it!" Roy exclaimed. "This is exactly the break I needed from the chaos of the city. Hold on, let me grab those beers from the fridge."

He returned with two chilled bottles, popped the caps, and they settled into reclining chairs by the pool, the cool glass condensation against their hands. Roy connected his phone to a wireless speaker, filling the air with mellow tunes.

A gentle sea breeze rustled through their hair, mingling with the calming sound of the waves and the distant cries of seagulls circling the shore. Everything felt perfect, idyllic. As they sipped their beers, Rick turned to Roy.

"So, how's Christina? Everything good between you two?"

"Yeah, everything's great. Why do you ask?"

"No reason, just asking. You've seemed a little… preoccupied lately, that's all."

Roy sighed softly. "It's not that I don't love Christina, because I do, deeply. But whenever I try to ask her about her family or her background, she gets… uncomfortable. She always changes the subject. Sometimes I can't help but wonder what's really going on and why she's hiding things from me."

Rick chuckled. "I bet your girlfriend's a spy! We need to run a background check on her."

Roy laughed, the tension easing slightly. "Yeah, maybe you're right."

After finishing their beers, they decided to take a stroll along the beach. They rolled up their long pants to their knees and walked towards the shore, relishing the cool touch of the ocean water on their feet. Standing at the water's edge, the waves washing over their ankles and receding, brought a sense of peaceful serenity. The soft sand yielded beneath their feet, the soothing rhythm of the sea washing away their worries. The entire experience was invigorating.

As they walked, two stunning girls approached them. One was blonde, the other a striking brunette, both radiating confidence in their sexy bikinis, their toned bodies catching the sunlight. The brunette had captivating blue eyes and curly hair, her bikini playfully revealing. The blonde, with piercing green eyes and straight hair, also wore an alluring bikini. They were undeniably eye-catching, and surprisingly, they were heading directly towards Roy and Rick. The brunette reached them first, a warm smile on her face.

"Hi, my name is Kate, and this is my friend Rachael. What are your names?"

"Hi, I'm Roy, and this is my friend Rick," Roy replied, returning her smile.

It seemed Kate, the brunette, was particularly interested in Roy.

"So, Roy," she said, her gaze lingering on him, "you and your friend are on vacation, I presume?"

"Yes, we are," Roy nodded.

Meanwhile, Rick seemed equally captivated by the blonde, Rachael. A mutual blush coloured their cheeks as their eyes met.

"Do you guys have any plans for tonight?" Kate asked. "We're getting a bit bored and don't have anything lined up."

"No plans at all," Roy replied. "We were just going to chill at my house. If you'd like, you're both welcome to join us." He gestured towards his house visible down the beach.

"That sounds like fun! By the way, Roy, your house looks absolutely beautiful. We'd love to spend some time with you both. How about seven PM?" Kate said, her voice enthusiastic.

They exchanged goodbyes, and Rick and Roy headed back to the house. Rick was visibly excited at the prospect of having two beautiful girls over, while Roy seemed a bit more conflicted, his thoughts turning to Christina.

"Hey Rick," Roy began hesitantly, "is it okay that we invited those two girls over? How would Christina feel if she found out?"

"Don't worry about it, brother," Rick said dismissively. "She won't know. And who said anything about sleeping with them? Just enjoy the company, it'll be a good time. We came here to relax, right? So, just enjoy hanging out with that brunette."

"I don't feel entirely right about this, Rick," Roy confessed. "It feels a bit like I'm cheating on Christina. I don't want to hurt her."

"Relax, man! No one will know. But if you're really that uncomfortable, let me call them and cancel."

"No, it's okay," Roy conceded with a sigh. "Let them come. I'll just make it clear I'm committed. Why should you ruin your chance with Rachael? She seems like a really nice girl."

Twilight painted the sky in hues of fiery orange as the sun began its descent towards the horizon. Roy and Rick sat on poolside recliners, silently enjoying the breath-taking sunset, a sense of peaceful contentment settling over them.

At six forty-five PM, Rick nudged Roy. "Hey, our guests will be here in a few minutes. Should we freshen up?"

"Oh, yeah, good idea," Roy agreed.

By seven-oh-five PM, the doorbell rang. Roy opened the door, and his eyes widened in surprise. Kate and Rachael stood before him, both dressed in stunning, figure-hugging one-piece dresses. Kate wore a shimmering black sequined number with a backless halter neck, while Rachael looked radiant in a striking navy blue one-shoulder dress. Roy was momentarily speechless.

"Hi Kate, Rachael," he finally managed, a hint of admiration in his voice. "You both look… wow! Please, come inside."

Kate and Rachael stepped into the house, their eyes taking in the elegant décor as they made their way to the living room.

"Roy, your house is gorgeous," Kate said, her smile warm. "Thanks for inviting us."

"Oh, it's my pleasure," Roy replied.

Rick, who had been waiting in the living room, blushed as Rachael entered. He stared at her, momentarily frozen by her glamorous appearance.

"Hi, Rachael," he stammered, "you look absolutely stunning tonight."

"Thank you," Rachael replied, her eyes sparkling. "You're looking quite dashing yourself, Rick."

Roy and Rick then gave Kate and Rachael a brief tour of the house. Afterwards, Roy, Kate, and Rachael settled onto the comfortable living room couch, while Rick headed to the kitchen to fetch beers for everyone. He returned with the chilled bottles, popped the tops, and they all clinked them together. "Cheers!"

Time drifted by in easy conversation. They ordered a feast from a nearby Italian restaurant – creamy Penne alla Vodka, crispy Toasted Ravioli, hearty Spaghetti and Meatballs, and an authentic wood-fired pizza. They gathered in the dining room, enjoying the delicious meal with glasses of fine wine. As dinner concluded, they moved back to the poolside in the backyard to relax. Kate paired off with Roy, and Rachael with Rick, each couple engaging in their own private conversation.

"So, Roy," Kate began, her eyes playfully assessing him, "are you single?"

"Hmm, nope," Roy replied honestly. "I'm in a relationship. My girlfriend's name is Christina. We're in college together. What about you? Are you single?"

"Yes, I am," Kate said. "I was in a relationship before, but it didn't work out, so we broke up."

"Tell me, how's your love life going?" Kate inquired.

"Well, it's going well," Roy said, a thoughtful expression on his face. "Who doesn't have their ups and downs, but all I can say is, right now, things are good."

As they talked, Kate subtly tried to get closer to Roy, a hopeful glint in her eyes. However, Roy, mindful of Christina, maintained a polite distance. Meanwhile, Rick and Rachael were clearly hitting it off, their conversation punctuated by laughter and lingering glances. Rick's arm rested casually across Rachael's back, their faces inches apart, the air thick with unspoken attraction. Soon enough, they were locked in a passionate kiss. Watching them, a sense of warmth stirred within Roy as Kate leaned closer, her hand gently finding his. They were about to share a moment when…

Chapter 5: Misunderstanding.

The air crackled with unspoken tension as Roy and Kate leaned in, the promise of a moment hanging between them. Suddenly, a voice sliced through the tranquil night.

"Roy! What the hell are you doing?"

Standing at the edge of the pool area, her silhouette framed by the soft outdoor lighting, was Christina. Fury radiated from her, her eyes blazing. Roy froze, his blood turning to ice. Christina's unexpected arrival shattered the intimate atmosphere, leaving a palpable sense of dread in its wake.

"Oh, Christina! Hi," Roy stammered, his face paling. "What are you doing here?"

"What am I doing here?" Christina's voice was sharp, each word laced with accusation. "Perhaps you should tell me what *you're* doing. And who are these girls?"

"Christina, this is Kate, and this is Rachael," Roy explained, his voice trembling slightly. "They just came over to hang out with us. Nothing's going on."

"Can we talk? Somewhere in private?" Christina's gaze remained fixed on Roy, unwavering.

"Yeah, sure. Let's go inside," Roy agreed, his heart pounding with apprehension.

They retreated into the kitchen, the silence between them thick with unspoken accusations.

"I'm sorry, Christina," Roy began, his eyes pleading. "It's not what it looks like. They just came over to hang out. We met them on the beach today, and I invited them back to the house."

"What? You invited *both* of them? What were you thinking, Roy? Did you really think I wouldn't understand what was happening here? You're cheating on me."

"No, Christina, you've got it all wrong," Roy insisted, his voice rising in desperation. "We were just talking. Rick's the one who was really hitting it off with Rachael. I already told Kate that I'm in a relationship. If you don't believe me, you can ask Rick and Kate. I even thought about canceling, but I didn't want Rick to miss out because of me. Please, trust me. Ask Rick."

Just then, Rick, followed by Kate and Rachael, entered the kitchen, sensing the charged atmosphere.

"Christina," Rick interjected, his expression earnest, "Roy's telling the truth. He actually suggested canceling the plan, but I was the one who insisted they come over."

Kate added her reassurance. "Christina, Roy told me all about you. He said how much he loves you and that he would never do anything to hurt your feelings."

Hearing their corroborating accounts, the tension visibly drained from Christina's face. Her shoulders relaxed, and a wave of relief washed over her.

"Oh," she said softly, her voice contrite. "I thought… I thought Roy was cheating on me. I'm so sorry, Roy, for doubting you."

"It's okay, Christina," Roy replied, his relief evident. "You don't have to apologize. I should have told you about our plans earlier. Anyway," he continued, changing the subject, "how did you even get here?"

"Well, I was getting bored at Grandma's, and you were only a couple of hours away. So, I thought I'd surprise you. And you certainly surprised me… at first," she admitted with a small smile. "When I arrived, the front door was already open, so I just walked right in."

"Oh, I must have forgotten to lock it by mistake," Roy said, a sheepish look on his face.

Around eleven-thirty PM, Kate and Rachael announced it was getting late and bid their goodbyes.

"Goodbye, Roy. Goodbye, Christina. Goodbye, Rick!" Kate called out.

"Goodbye, Rick," Rachael added, her eyes lingering on him. "Don't forget to call me tomorrow. We might have to finish what we started tonight," she said with a playful blush before she and Kate departed.

Roy and Christina retreated to their bedroom. After settling into bed, Roy turned to Christina, his voice filled with sincerity.

"Hey, I love you. I would never intentionally hurt you. Please, trust me. I would never do anything that would make you feel that way."

"I love you too, Roy," Christina replied, her gaze soft. "But the picture I walked in on… anyone would have been furious."

"I know, Christina. Just forget about it. The only thing that matters is that you're here. You're the best thing that's ever happened to me. I love you."

"The feeling is mutual, Roy."

They embraced, a tender hug that dissolved into a passionate kiss, their connection reaffirming the bond between them, making the rest of the night a cherished memory.

Months passed, marked by the quiet rhythm of their deepening relationship and the looming end of their university years. On their final day, Roy, Christina, and Rick sat together in a familiar corridor, a bittersweet melancholy hanging in the air. Leaving the carefree days of college, the camaraderie of friends, and the echoes of shared laughter was a poignant prospect. A nervous anticipation for the "real world," with its unpredictable future, mingled with the sadness of parting. Yet, beneath the surface, a current of hope persisted – the hope of carving successful paths, wherever life might lead. A wave of nostalgia washed over them as they reminisced about late-night study sessions, their favourite professors' quirks, the sun-drenched afternoons on campus, and the fleeting moments that would never quite be replicated. All they could carry forward were the indelible memories and the unwavering hope for a bright future.

Convocation day arrived, a sea of black academic gowns and square hats filling the ceremonial hall. Excitement buzzed through the graduating students, a collective sense of accomplishment tinged with the nervous flutter of facing the unknown. A panel of esteemed professors and the principal sat on the stage, a silent testament to their years of guidance. The moment arrived when Dean Edward Williams approached the microphone. His voice, warm and resonant, filled the hall as he delivered an inspiring speech, encouraging the students to embrace the future with courage and resilience. He concluded with a heartfelt blessing.

"May you all be successful in life and achieve all of your desired goals. I wish you the best of luck in navigating the challenges that lie ahead. May God grant you the strength and wisdom to make the difficult choices in your careers. God bless you all, and thank you."

The ceremony commenced, each student's name announced, a symbolic passage onto the stage to receive their hard-earned degree and a congratulatory medal. Rick's name was called first among their trio. He bounded to the stage, his excitement radiating as he accepted his degree and posed for a photograph with the dean. A few students later, Christina's name echoed through the hall. She gracefully accepted her degree, a proud smile on her face as she too posed for the camera. Finally, Roy's name was announced. He walked to the stage, a sense of quiet satisfaction settling over him as he received his degree and medal. Then, to the surprise of many, he requested permission from the dean to address the graduating class. Dean Williams nodded his assent. Roy approached the microphone, adjusted it thoughtfully, and began.

"Hello, friends."

A murmur of surprise rippled through the audience. No one had anticipated a speech from Roy.

He continued, his voice steady and sincere, "I know this is our last day within these familiar walls. Leaving behind the tapestry of good memories we've woven here is undoubtedly bittersweet. We've shared experiences that will likely shape us for a lifetime. Some of us found our first love within these grounds, others forged bonds of friendship as strong as family, and many of us learned invaluable life lessons. Whatever wisdom we've gleaned here, it's our responsibility to make our professors, our families, and ourselves proud by contributing positively to our society, our country, and by striving to make the world a slightly better place. The future will undoubtedly present challenges, moments of insecurity, stress, and fear in the face of unforeseen circumstances. But you know what? That's inevitable; we can't control everything. What we *can* control is our response. We must trust ourselves, lean on our families and friends, remain loyal to our work, and face our responsibilities with a smile. I am confident that success will follow. I pray that all your dreams come to fruition, that you all achieve the goals you've set for yourselves. Best of luck, and thank you."

A wave of enthusiastic applause filled the hall as Roy concluded his speech, a mixture of joy and poignant emotion hanging in the air.

After the ceremony, the graduates spilled into the corridor, congratulating each other, a bittersweet farewell hanging in their words. It was a moment of both exhilaration and sadness, a final gathering before paths diverged into the unknown. Roy, however, seemed genuinely happy. He embraced Christina, kissed her tenderly, and they posed for a photograph, their degrees held aloft like trophies.

Roy had officially earned his degree in "Human Psychology." The entire graduating class then gathered for a group photo, a collective effort to freeze this pivotal moment in time, creating a memory to last a lifetime. As the sound of the camera's click echoed, the students spontaneously removed their square hats and tossed them into the sky, a symbolic end to one chapter and the hopeful beginning of another.

Roy had made a significant decision about his future some time ago, applying the previous month to join the rigorous training program for the Navy SEALs. He had hesitated to tell Christina, fearing her reaction. After the convocation ceremony, Roy and Christina returned to his house, both feeling the exhaustion of the day's events. They took refreshing showers and settled onto the comfortable couch.

"Roy," Christina began, her voice soft, "our studies are finally over. Everything's going to be so different now. We won't be able to spend as much time together as we did at university."

"Christina, don't worry, darling," Roy reassured her, taking her hand. "We'll still find time for each other. But hey, there's something important I need to tell you. You have to promise me you won't get mad after you hear it."

"What is it, Roy?"

"Christina, I've decided to go for military training at the Naval Special Warfare Preparatory School in Great Lakes, Illinois."

"What! You're joining the military? When did you decide this? You didn't even tell me!" Her voice was a mixture of shock and hurt.

"No, it's not like that," Roy explained quickly. "I was going to tell you as soon as I got confirmation, and I just received the acceptance letter this morning."

Furious, Christina retorted, "Why would you hide something like this from me? You should have told me earlier, Roy! You've really broken my heart. How are we supposed to be together when you're off in the military? Long-distance relationships don't work, Roy. Try to understand. I really love you, and I want to spend my whole life with you."

"Christina, I love you too," Roy pleaded, "but please understand. This training is something I really want to do. I want to serve my country. Please try to see it from my perspective. I've always wanted to join the special forces. It will push me, both physically and mentally. This is what I feel I need to do. Please understand, Christina."

"Yes, I understand, Roy," Christina said, her voice trembling with unshed tears. "But what about me? What am I supposed to do without you? How will I know if you're okay? I'll just be constantly worried and stressed. I don't think this is going to work, Roy. I think… I think we're done."

Christina grabbed her purse and walked towards the door.

"Wait! Christina, please don't go," Roy cried out, his voice filled with desperation. "Please don't leave me. You're the best thing that's ever happened to me. I won't be able to forget you. Christina, please understand."

"If you cared so much about me, then why are you leaving?" she asked, her eyes glistening. "Just stay here."

"Trust me, Christina," Roy pleaded. "We'll be alright. We can make this work."

"No, Roy," she said, her voice final. "I'm leaving."

And with that, she walked out of Roy's house, leaving him standing there, devastated. Tears welled in his eyes as he replayed all the cherished moments he had shared with Christina.

Roy reached for a bottle of scotch, seeking solace in its numbing embrace. He drank until the edges of his pain began to blur. Grief washed over him, a heavy weight of regret for the difficult choice he had made between his love for Christina and his lifelong ambition. Choosing career over love left him with a profound sense of sorrow, each memory of their time together a sharp reminder of what he might have lost.

The doorbell rang, jolting Roy from his drunken stupor. He stumbled to the door and pulled it open to find Rick standing there.

"Rick? What are you doing here? It's midnight!"

"I've been calling you since eight PM, Roy, must have been ten times. You weren't picking up. I got worried something had happened, so I came over to check on you. And what happened to *you*? Why are you so drunk and the place is a mess?"

"Rick, my friend," Roy slurred, his voice thick with despair, "I'm devastated."

"What are you saying, Roy? What happened?"

"Christina broke up with me. She left."

"What? You guys broke up?" Rick's voice was incredulous. "Don't tell me she didn't take the news about you joining the military well."

"No," Roy choked out, tears welling in his eyes again. "I told her today. I tried to explain why I wanted to do this, but she just couldn't understand. I tried so hard, Rick, but she still left me. I'm really broken, man."

Tears streamed down Roy's face.

"Hey, buddy, don't cry," Rick said, his voice gentle. "You're a strong guy. She should have tried to understand your situation, Roy. Don't worry, I'm here for you. Everything will be alright.

Just try to relax and get some sleep. You look exhausted. I'll come by again tomorrow to check on you."

Rick handed Roy a glass of water, urged him to go to bed, and then quietly left.

The next day, Roy received a text message from Christina.

"Hey Roy, I know you love me so much, and I love you too, deeply. But I can't see this relationship working with such a long distance between us. I thought about trying, but I honestly believe it would eventually fail, and the heartbreak would be even worse. So, I think it's better to end it now, even though it hurts terribly. I know you care about me, and I doubt I'll ever find someone like you again. But we have to accept this, Roy. I'm so sorry if I've hurt you. I truly hope you achieve everything you dream of in your life. I don't know if we'll ever meet again. Just want to say goodbye one last time. Love you. I hope you'll understand."

Chapter 6: Introduction to The Navy SEAL.

September arrived, marking the beginning of a new chapter in Roy's life. Veronica, a mix of pride and apprehension, helped him pack his bags for the long and arduous journey of Navy SEAL training. She was overjoyed to see Roy embracing responsibility and pursuing a challenging path, yet a mother's worry gnawed at her, fearing for his safety and well-being.

The next morning, Veronica accompanied Roy to the airport. As they said their goodbyes, she offered a heartfelt blessing.

"Son, please take care of yourself. Don't get into any unnecessary trouble. Best of luck, and make your father proud."

"Don't worry, Mom," Roy reassured her, his voice a blend of excitement and determination. "I'll be alright. I'll make Dad proud, I promise. I'll call you as soon as I arrive. Take care, goodbye."

They embraced, a silent exchange of love and support, and Roy walked towards the gate, a complex mix of emotions swirling within him. The thrill of embarking on a new adventure warred with the sadness of leaving his loved ones behind. It was a poignant transition, a step into the unknown. An hour later, he boarded his plane, soaring towards the next demanding phase of his life.

Roy arrived at Great Lakes, Illinois, the starting point of his Navy SEAL training. He joined approximately 40 other aspiring candidates, all vying for a place in this elite force. The first hurdle was a rigorous SEAL Physical Screening Assignment, demanding they exceed minimum performance standards in a series of gruelling tests.

These minimum requirements included a 500-yard swim using breaststroke or combat sidestroke in under 12 minutes and 30 seconds (with a competitive time of 9 minutes or less), at least 50 push-ups in 2 minutes (with a best count of 90 or more), at least 50 sit-ups in 2 minutes (with a best count of 90 or more), at least ten pull-ups from a dead hang (with a competitive count of 18 or more), and a 1.5-mile run in pants and boots in under 10 minutes and 30 seconds (with a competitive time of 9 minutes and 30 seconds or less).

Roy, driven by his determination, surpassed the minimum requirements with impressive results. However, not all candidates were successful. Only 25 out of the initial 40 passed the screening, earning the right to continue to the next stage: an eight-week preparatory training program designed to hone the physical capabilities of aspiring SEALs. This phase began with a challenging Physical Test and culminated in an even more demanding one, consisting of a timed four-mile run and a timed 1,000-meter swim. The training pushed Roy to his limits, testing his mental and physical endurance.

"These exercises are far more brutal than I anticipated," he thought, his muscles screaming in protest. "This is truly testing my patience. Whatever it takes, I have to pass this. This is a challenge I must conquer."

Amidst the gruelling training, Roy found an unexpected source of support in a fellow candidate named Eric Thompson. They forged a strong bond, their shared struggles creating a sense of camaraderie.

As the sixth week of training drew to a close, Roy, Eric, and the remaining candidates returned to their dorms, exhausted and battered. They sought solace in familiar routines: some collapsed onto their bunk beds, some called home for comfort, and others engaged in light-hearted banter, seeking a brief respite from the relentless pressure of the day.

Roy settled onto his bunk, his bed positioned beneath Eric's.

"What are you up to, bro?" Roy asked, noticing Eric engrossed in a book.

"Nothing much, just reading," Eric replied.

"Don't you feel completely drained after training?"

"Yeah, I do. But reading helps me unwind. It calms my nerves."

"Oh, any steamy scenes in that book?" Roy teased.

"I think there's one, yeah. One of my friends who's already read it told me," Eric chuckled.

"Now I understand how reading helps you relieve stress," Roy joked.

They shared a laugh, bid each other goodnight, and drifted off to sleep, bracing themselves for the challenges that awaited them the next day.

Through sheer grit and unwavering determination, Roy and Eric, along with a select few other candidates, successfully completed the demanding eight-week preparatory program. They were now ready to advance to the next, even more formidable, 24-week training program: Basic Underwater Demolition/SEAL (BUD/S).

"Bro, we finally made it through the first stage," Roy said, a sense of accomplishment in his voice.

"Yeah," Eric replied, his brow furrowed with concern, "but I'm a bit worried about this next 24-week program. I've heard it's incredibly tough, and not everyone makes it through."

"Don't worry, we'll get through it together," Roy reassured him, his eyes filled with determination. "I know we will."

They were then transferred to Coronado, California, the location for their next phase of training: Indoctrination (INDOC), a gruelling three-week introduction to the world of BUD/S. Navy SEAL instructors wasted no time in pushing the candidates to their limits, subjecting them to intense physical training, obstacle courses, and a barrage of unique and demanding exercises. This phase was specifically designed to prepare candidates for the relentless challenges of the first phase of BUD/S. It proved to be an arduous test for both Roy and Eric.

"Man, this is exhausting," Roy groaned, his body aching. "I have a feeling it's only going to get tougher from here."

"Of course, it is, bro," Eric agreed, his voice firm. "We have to make our will stronger than ever if we want to succeed."

Driven by their unwavering resolve, they persevered, completing the introductory three weeks and qualifying for Phase One: Physical Conditioning, a brutal seven-week gauntlet.

The first phase of BUD/S was designed to assess the candidates' physical conditioning, water competency, teamwork skills, and mental fortitude. Trainees were required to swim long distances with 50-pound weights, push their bodies to the breaking point with running, swimming, and calisthenics, and endure increasingly demanding training regimens as the weeks progressed. They participated in weekly four-mile timed runs in boots and pants, navigated gruelling obstacle courses, swam up to two miles in the ocean wearing fins, and learned the intricacies of small boat seamanship.

The first two weeks of basic conditioning served as a brutal prelude to the infamous "Hell Week," the third week of Phase One. During this five-and-a-half-day ordeal, SEAL candidates were subjected to continuous, rigorous training, often deprived of sleep for more than four hours for the entire week. They ran over 200 miles and endured approximately 20 hours of intense physical training per day.

The remaining four weeks focused on acquiring essential skills in hydrographic surveying and chart creation. Due to the extreme demands of this phase, many candidates began to question their decision to join the program, leading to a significant number choosing to "Drop on Request." This tradition involved placing one's helmet liner next to a designated pole with a brass ship's bell attached and ringing the bell three times, a symbolic act of surrender. It has also been reported that all candidates receive two comprehensive medical examinations within 24 hours after the gruelling ordeal of Hell Week.

One day, towards the end of the fifth week, Roy sat on his bunk, his gaze fixed on a photograph of his mother. Eric approached him, glancing at the image on his phone.

"Hey, whose photo is that?" Eric asked.

"It's my mother," Roy replied, his voice tinged with longing. "I really miss her, you know. Today, during training, I was so frustrated that I almost quit. But then, the image of my mother and father flashed through my mind, and it gave me the strength to keep going. My father was a fearless soul, you know. He designed some of the weapons we're using right now. He was a brilliant inventor and dedicated his life to serving the U.S. military. Now, it's my turn to serve my country."

"I didn't know that, Roy," Eric said, his voice filled with admiration. "That's incredibly brave of you. I'm sure we'll both make it through this program, and you'll definitely make your father proud."

Finally, the last day of the training program arrived. Eric and Roy, battered but unbowed, had successfully completed Phase

One. They embraced, congratulating each other on achieving this significant milestone.

The next challenge was Phase Two: Combat Diving, a demanding seven-week program designed to transform SEAL candidates into competent and proficient combat swimmers. During this phase, the intensity of the physical training continued to escalate. The focus shifted to diving physics, underwater skills, and combat SCUBA. Candidates learned to master two types of SCUBA: open circuit (compressed air) and closed circuit. They also received training in essential dive medicine and basic medical skills. Emphasis was placed on long-distance underwater dives, training students to become effective combat divers, utilizing swimming and diving techniques as their primary means of transportation from their launch point to their combat objective. This skill set is what truly distinguished SEALs from other United States Special Forces.

At the end of Phase Two, candidates were required to complete a timed two-mile swim with fins in 80 minutes, a four-mile run in boots in 31 minutes, and gruelling 3.5-mile and 5.5-mile swims. Successful candidates demonstrated exceptional comfort in the water and an unwavering ability to perform under extreme stress and in harsh, uncomfortable environments. Candidates who were not entirely at ease in the water often struggled to succeed.

Throughout this challenging phase, Roy and Eric continued to support and motivate each other, their camaraderie proving to be a vital source of strength. Week after week, they pushed themselves to the limit, eventually completing Phase Two, along with a handful of other determined candidates. After completing the training for the day, Roy sat alone on a bench outside his room, a wave of longing washing over him as he gazed at Christina's photo on his phone.

"I really miss her," he thought, his heart aching. "Should I call her? Would it be okay?"

Torn between his desire to connect with her and the uncertainty of their situation, he hesitated. After several minutes of internal debate, he finally mustered the courage to dial her number. However, the call went unanswered. Her phone appeared to be switched off.

"Her battery probably died," he reasoned, trying to quell his disappointment. "I'll try again tomorrow."

The next morning, as soon as he woke up, he dialled Christina's number again. But the result was the same: the phone remained switched off.

"Is she alright?" he wondered, a flicker of worry in his eyes. "Did she change her number? I guess she must have. I'll try to find her after I finish training."

The beginning of Phase Three, Land Warfare, marked another significant step in their journey. This seven-week phase focused on mastering essential skills in weapons handling, patrolling, marksmanship, infantry tactics, rappelling, land navigation, and small unit tactics. The class was taught how to process all the information necessary to successfully complete a wide range of missions.

Alongside the demanding physical training, the curriculum incorporated extensive classroom work, covering compass navigation, basic weapon proficiency, and land navigation techniques. These skills were designed to help the class transition from novice trainees to confident and capable operators in the field. The pace of learning accelerated rapidly during this phase.

For the final five weeks of training, the class was transported offshore, approximately 60 miles from Coronado, to San Clemente Island. On the island, they put into practice all the skills they had acquired during the third phase. The days became longer and more work-intensive, mirroring the gruelling hours spent in real-world operational scenarios. Many students considered this to be one of the toughest parts of the entire training program, as they were required to endure relentless training seven days a week, with minimal sleep, all while handling live ammunition and explosives. The interaction with instructors was constant and intense, and punishments for errors reached their most severe levels yet. By the end of the third phase, candidates were required to complete a timed two-mile ocean swim with fins in 75 minutes, a four-mile timed run in boots in 30 minutes, and a gruelling 14-mile run.

Roy struggled to complete the tasks, his senses often overwhelmed by fatigue and stress. Yet, the memory of his father, his unwavering courage and dedication, served as a powerful source of strength and motivation. He pushed himself beyond his limits, drawing inspiration from his father's legacy. Finally, after immense effort, he completed the demanding requirements of Phase Three.

With the completion of this phase, the focus shifted to acquiring more advanced tactical skills, the final polish needed to become a fully-fledged Navy SEAL. Roy moved to San Diego, CA, for a three-week program at Parachute Jump School. Here, he underwent intensive training in both static line and free-fall techniques at Tactical Air Operations. This accelerated program, facilitated by world-class instructors, was designed to develop safe and proficient free-fall jumpers in a short period.

Having successfully completed the training at Parachute Jump School, Roy embarked on the last and most critical stage of his journey: SEAL Qualification Training (SQT), a rigorous 26-week course. This program was designed to elevate students from a fundamental understanding of Naval Special Warfare to a more advanced level of tactical proficiency. SQT provided students with the core tactical knowledge they would need to join a SEAL Platoon.

Roy learned advanced skill sets in close-quarters combat, small unit tactics, land navigation, weapons training, unarmed combat, demolitions, cold-weather operations in Kodiak, Alaska, maritime operations, and medical skills.

Before graduation, all students were required to attend Survival, Evasion, Resistance, and Escape (SERE) training. Graduation from SQT culminated in the awarding of the coveted Navy SEAL Trident and the designation of Navy Enlisted Classification 5326 Combatant Swimmer or Special Warfare Officer (SEAL).

New SEALs were then assigned to a SEAL Team at Coronado, CA, or Little Creek, VA, and began advanced training in preparation for their first deployment. This pre-deployment workup typically lasted for 12 to 18 months and was divided into three distinct phases. Roy and Eric were both assigned to SEAL TEAM 3, specializing in Middle East operations. Roy felt a sense of belonging, a sense of camaraderie with his new "family."

Chapter 7: Operation NIGHTHAWK.

A palpable sense of dread hung over the United States. The threat of enemy attacks loomed, casting a long shadow over the nation. The CIA and Homeland Security worked tirelessly, a united front against an invisible enemy, searching for any flicker of suspicious activity that could lead to catastrophe.

The CIA intercepted a chilling exchange between a terrorist operative and their handler. The Al-Qaeda terrorist group in Afghanistan was plotting another attack on U.S. soil. Dozens of CIA spies, embedded deep within the terrorist network, fed a stream of crucial information, vital for averting disaster. The President convened an emergency meeting at the White House, the air thick with tension, as top officials grappled with the imminent threat. The decision was made: a surgical strike, a swift and decisive blow to cripple the enemy's heart in Afghanistan, would be launched in two weeks. The military and the CIA would join forces, their expertise meshing to execute this high-stakes operation.

SEAL Team 3 was chosen for the mission, their reputation for precision and effectiveness preceding them. Simon Smith, the team's seasoned leader, collaborated closely with Richard King, the CIA's Head of Operations, a man known for his sharp intellect and unwavering resolve. Richard's track record in similar operations was impeccable, his bold decisions often the key to success. Simon, a veteran of countless missions in the Middle East, possessed an intimate understanding of the region's terrorist organizations, his team's success built on meticulous planning and a zero-casualty record.

The CIA christened the mission "NIGHTHAWK," a code name that echoed the stealth and precision required.

Richard received a critical piece of intelligence: Mohammad Suleiman, Al-Qaeda's second-in-command, the architect of the impending attack, was hiding in a heavily guarded three-story safe house in Kabul, Afghanistan. The safe house, located near the bustling Kabul water tank in the Sarak-E-Kabul Charikar district, was a fortress. Classified information revealed Suleiman's operations were conducted from the third floor, a level fortified with an army of 25 armed terrorists. The third floor, sealed off from the outside world, offered no visual access, making any direct assault a deadly gamble.

The Kabul water tank area, a vibrant hub teeming with a local bazaar, presented a logistical nightmare. The only viable window for an attack was at the stroke of midnight, 03:00 hours, when the streets would be deserted. The extraction plan was equally perilous: an airlift from the building's terrace was the only option. The entire operation demanded meticulous planning, a flawless execution to avoid catastrophic casualties. Richard tasked one of his deep-cover assets within Al-Qaeda to secure the safe house's blueprints. Two days later, a detailed schematic arrived, revealing the exact positions of guards, their weaponry, and every potential vulnerability.

Simon and Richard, working in perfect sync, constructed a full-scale replica of the safe house, a training ground where every detail mirrored the real target. They crafted a meticulously choreographed plan to neutralize the threat with maximum efficiency, a tight 20-minute window for the entire operation, including the extraction. The training began immediately, each team member navigating the replica building, eliminating simulated threats. Every obstacle, every potential danger was meticulously recreated, a constant reminder of the razor's edge they would walk. For Roy and Eric, this was their baptism by fire, their first mission, and the weight of responsibility pressed heavily on their shoulders.

"Eric, this is intense," Roy confessed, his voice tight with nerves. "I'm not sure I can memorize the whole plan."

"Yeah, I know what you mean," Eric replied, his brow furrowed. "But I think after a few more runs, we'll get it."

"Yeah, you're right," Roy agreed, forcing a note of confidence into his voice.

With each repetition, their movements became more fluid, their accuracy sharpening. Richard and his team, meanwhile, monitored the real safe house around the clock, utilizing live satellite feeds and intel from their ground spy team. Every piece of information, every subtle shift in the target's routine, was analyzed and integrated into the plan.

Tuesday arrived, just one week before the scheduled mission. Another meeting convened at the White House, the President and his top advisors gathered in the tense atmosphere of the Situation Room. Operation NIGHTHAWK, shrouded in secrecy, was a closely guarded secret, its timing known only to a select few. The complete operational blueprint was presented to the President, along with a detailed contingency plan, Plan B, to be activated if the situation deteriorated. After careful consideration, the President gave the green light, authorizing the mission. At his request, the entire operation would be streamed live to the White House, a silent witness to the unfolding drama.

Simon and Richard finalized the mission's details, a symphony of precision and calculated risk. Simon then briefed his team, his voice calm and authoritative.

"Boys, we're being transported to Bagram Military Base in Afghanistan. For the mission, we'll be traveling in four tinted civilian vehicles, to avoid detection. The sniper will eliminate the four exterior guards. We'll then neutralize all interior threats within exactly 20 minutes, followed by an airlift extraction from the roof. Two choppers will be waiting for us."

"When is this happening, sir?" Roy asked, his voice betraying a hint of anticipation.

"Exactly seven days from today," Simon replied, his gaze sweeping across the room. "Are we clear, boys?"

"Yes, sir!" the team responded in unison.

That same day, Roy and Eric shared dinner with their teammates, a final moment of camaraderie before the storm. David, a seasoned veteran, clapped Roy on the shoulder.

"What's up, bro? Excited? Or scared?"

"Hmmm, a little of both, to be honest," Roy admitted. "More nervous than scared, I guess. It's my first mission."

"It's okay to be nervous," David reassured him. "I was a wreck on my first mission. But we got through it, and we'll get through this. We've got each other's backs."

"Yeah, thanks," Roy said, a small smile playing on his lips.

Beneath the surface of bravado and resolve, a current of nervous energy coursed through the team. The mission date loomed, a dark cloud on the horizon.

Saturday, three days before the mission, the team was transported to the airport. A massive C17 Globemaster, its wings stretching like a giant bird of prey, waited for them. They boarded, along with their equipment, and were flown to Bagram Military Base in Afghanistan.

They arrived on time, the Afghan summer sun beating down on the sprawling base. Roy stepped off the plane, his eyes taking in the scene for the first time. The base bustled with activity: marines tending to cargo, soldiers engaged in rigorous drills, the air thick with the purpose and dedication of those sworn to protect their nation. The temperature hovered around a comfortable 75°F, a deceptive calm before the impending storm.

Roy and his teammates were directed to their dorms, instructed to rest before a crucial briefing scheduled for 17:00 hours. They grabbed a quick lunch, Roy savouring his favourite spaghetti and beef stew with mashed potatoes, a brief moment of normalcy before the chaos. At 17:00 hours, they gathered for the briefing, the atmosphere charged with anticipation. Simon's voice cut through the tension.

"These are the live feeds of the target safe house, where Suleiman is hiding. And these are the photographs of all the terrorists guarding the building. Memorize them."

They were given a thorough review of the extraction plan, and instructed to gather any intelligence that could help them dismantle the Al-Qaeda network.

That night, the team relaxed around a crackling bonfire, the flickering flames casting dancing shadows on their faces. They shared stories, cracked jokes, a desperate attempt to find levity in the face of the unknown. Roy sat beside Simon, the team leader's presence a source of quiet strength.

"So, what's your story, pretty boy?" Simon asked, a hint of a smile on his lips.

"Well, I grew up in New York with my mom and dad. Dad was a famous scientist, invented a lot of high-tech weapons. He was murdered in his office because of one of his inventions, and the killer was never caught. Mom raised me. I got a degree in psychology, then went straight for Navy SEAL training."

"You seem like you come from money. How did you end up in the Navy SEALs?"

"My father dedicated his life to serving the nation, through his inventions. Now it's my turn to serve."

"I'm impressed," Simon said, his eyes reflecting the firelight. "I saw your skills in training. You have a gift for reading people, for anticipating the enemy's next move. You're going to be a great asset to this team."

"Thanks, Chief," Roy replied, a surge of pride coursing through him. "I'll do my best."

Sunday, two days before the mission, Roy immersed himself in the video feeds and photographs of the safe house. He studied the guards' routines, their mannerisms, their vulnerabilities, searching for any detail that could give them an edge.

The day of the mission arrived, heavy with anticipation. The operation was scheduled for that night. Simon addressed the team, the briefing room silent save for his measured words. The live satellite feed of the safe house played on the screen, a constant reminder of the danger that awaited them.

"Boys, remember everything from training. This is the real deal. Be cautious. Memorize every face, every detail. Your target is Suleiman. And don't forget to collect any evidence: computers, laptops, hard drives, anything that can help us dismantle Al-Qaeda. Is everyone clear?"

"Clear, sir!" the team roared in response.

"Alright, everyone, get some rest, clear your minds. We move out at 01:30 hours. Dismissed."

The team dispersed to their dorms, the silence broken only by the low hum of nervous energy. Eric turned to Roy, his voice hushed.

"A bit tense about the mission, bro."

"Don't worry, we'll be alright," Roy reassured him, though his own heart pounded in his chest. "We'll make this a success. It's okay to be scared, I am too. But I trust Simon, I trust the team. We'll get through this. Now get some rest. It's going to be a long night."

Midnight struck, and the team began their final preparations. They donned their bulletproof vests, checked their weapons, loaded extra magazines, secured their knives, and tucked grenades into their pockets. They holstered their handguns and equipped their night-vision goggles. An hour remained, a tense countdown to the unknown. They grabbed a quick meal, fuelling their bodies for the coming battle.

The atmosphere was thick with anticipation, a "calm before the storm" stillness. Some stared at photographs of loved ones, a silent prayer on their lips. Others sat with their eyes closed, seeking inner peace. A few attempted jokes, a fragile shield against the fear. Finally, the clock struck 01:30 hours. Operation NIGHTHAWK was a go.

Four black, bulletproof SUVs with tinted windows waited outside. The team piled into the vehicles, Roy and Eric sharing the same ride. The convoy sped towards Kabul, the silence inside the cars broken only by the rumble of the engines. The weight of their mission pressed down on them, the lives of their countrymen resting on their shoulders.

At the base, Richard and his team monitored the target location with unwavering focus, their eyes glued to the live satellite feed. They were in constant communication with their asset near the safe house, receiving real-time updates. At CIA headquarters in Langley, officials coordinated with Richard, the live feed of the mission transmitted directly to the White House. The President, along with his top advisors, watched the unfolding events from the war room, every step scrutinized, every decision weighed.

At 02:45 hours, the SEAL team entered Kabul, the target a mere 15 minutes away. The streets were deserted, only a handful of vehicles and pedestrians visible. The low rumble of the engines amplified the silence within the vehicles, each member of the team grappling with the gravity of the situation. In minutes, they reached their drop-off point, 300 meters from the safe house, a distance chosen to minimize the risk of detection. The four SUVs were positioned a mile away, a backup extraction plan in case the airlift failed.

The team advanced towards the target, their movements fluid and practiced. They reached the building, a cluster of nondescript houses surrounding an open area. A large water tank loomed eight blocks away. The team's sniper, a ghost in the night, scaled the water tank using a pre-positioned ladder. Reaching the top, he deployed his night-vision binoculars, his eyes scanning the target. He identified the exterior guards: one at the main door, two on the second floor, and one guarding the entrance to the third.

A thermal imaging drone, deployed by the CIA, provided a bird's-eye view of the safe house, revealing the interior layout. 21 armed men guarded the building: seven on the ground floor, nine on the second, and five on the third. The drone identified a lone figure sleeping on the third floor, likely their target, Mohammad Suleiman. The information was relayed to Simon.

"Sniper, take your shot when ready," Simon's voice crackled through the comms.

The sniper focused on the guard at the main door.

"Target in sight, sir."

"Okay, shoot."

A single shot echoed through the night. The guard slumped to the ground. The sniper swiftly shifted his aim to the second floor, eliminating the two guards with millisecond precision. He then targeted the guard on the third floor. Another shot, another kill.

"Four guards neutralized," the sniper reported.

Simon, followed by Roy, Eric, and the rest of the team, moved towards the safe house, their footsteps silent on the deserted streets. The sniper descended from the water tank and re-joined the team. They spread out, hugging the walls of the building, their weapons raised. The front door, reinforced with iron, was their next obstacle. The team's explosive expert deployed a small breaching charge, attaching it to the door.

"Breaching in three, two, one… BOOM!"

The explosion ripped through the night, tearing the door from its hinges.

The blast alerted the terrorists inside, chaos erupting within the building. Gunfire erupted from the entrance, three guards firing blindly into the night. Simon, leading the charge with two SEALs, tossed a grenade into the doorway. The explosion silenced the gunfire, eliminating the three guards. They stormed into the building, eight men, including Roy and Eric, taking the stairs, the remaining eight securing the ground floor. The air filled with the deafening roar of gunfire. A barrage of bullets rained down from the last room on the ground floor. The team took cover, returning fire. One teammate kicked down the door, two SEALs rushing into the room, their weapons spitting death. Four terrorists fell.

The house was a maze of rooms, a chaotic labyrinth. Roy and seven teammates cleared the first floor, then faced a hail of bullets from the second-floor entrance. Roy, his nerves steady, pulled the pin on a grenade and tossed it towards the enemy position. The explosion silenced the gunfire, allowing the team to breach the second floor. Six small rooms lined the hallway. They cleared each room systematically, kicking down doors, weapons ready. They breached two rooms, finding them empty. A sound from the third room alerted them. One teammate kicked down the door, another rushing in, his weapon blazing. One terrorist down. Suddenly, heavy gunfire erupted from the fifth room. A teammate tossed a grenade, disarming the enemy. Three SEALs stormed the room, eliminating five armed terrorists.

While three SEALs secured the second floor, the remaining five, including Roy and Eric, ascended the stairs to the third floor. The stairwell was a dark tunnel, their night-vision goggles their only guide. As they reached the third-floor landing, a grenade exploded at the entrance, forcing them to a halt. Roy, thinking fast, fired a grenade from his launcher, neutralizing any potential threats beyond the doorway. Simon, followed by Roy, led the charge onto the third floor. They began clearing the rooms. The first door they opened revealed Mohammad Suleiman cowering in a corner, a Glock clutched in his trembling hand. Simon fired three shots into Suleiman's chest. He died instantly. As Simon fired, four terrorists burst into the room, weapons raised. The team took cover, returning fire. Roy and Eric, their training kicking in, worked in perfect synchronicity, unleashing a deadly barrage. The four terrorists fell, their bodies joining the growing carnage. The third floor was a scene of devastation, blood spattered across the walls, bodies strewn across the floor. Simon ordered the team to search for evidence. Suleiman's body was placed in a body bag, and photographs were taken.

In the White House war room, the President watched the live feed, a grim satisfaction washing over him as he witnessed the death of Mohammad Suleiman. The mission was nearing completion. The team recovered five computers, extracting the hard drives as evidence. Roy, searching the room adjacent to Suleiman's, discovered a secret compartment beneath the floor. He kicked it open, revealing a hidden bag. Inside, he found a laptop and a USB drive.

"I found a hidden bag, Chief," Roy reported over the comms. "It contains a laptop and a USB drive."

"Well done, Roy! Take it and meet me on the roof. Our chopper is arriving in 120 seconds."

Simon, using his radio, ordered everyone to the roof.

"Everyone, get to the roof, fast! Chopper ETA is 120 seconds!"

As they waited, the sound of gunfire erupted from below. Someone had alerted the remaining terrorists. Richard, monitoring the situation from the base, relayed the urgent message.

"15 armed men are approaching the building. Evacuate immediately!"

The team opened fire from the roof, unleashing a hail of bullets. They hurled five grenades down, one exploding near a terrorist vehicle, killing four. The distinct whirring of helicopter blades reached their ears, a beacon of hope. Two choppers descended onto the roof. Eight SEALs, carrying Suleiman's body, boarded the first chopper, the remaining team members boarding the second. Each SEAL, as they boarded, kept their weapon trained on the doorway, ready to eliminate any last-minute threats.

As the choppers lifted off, four or five terrorists reached the roof, firing wildly. Miraculously, no shots hit the choppers, and they soared into the night

Chapter 8: Operation TORA BORA.

Three years had passed since Roy's gruelling introduction to the world of Navy SEALs. He and his team had become a finely-honed instrument, executing numerous operations across the rugged terrain of Afghanistan with lethal efficiency. Stationed at Bagram U.S. Military Base, their expertise in the region was undeniable. It was a typical Monday morning; Roy rose at 5:00 AM, his body already accustomed to the demanding rhythm of his daily exercises. Two hours of intense physical exertion later, he showered, refreshed, and headed to the mess hall for breakfast. As he ate, his attention drifted to the television screen displaying the morning news. Suddenly, a breaking news bulletin flashed across the screen.

"Four U.S. reporters have been taken hostage by Al-Qaeda. The terrorists are demanding the release of their top commander, Abu Hasan, as ransom."

A jolt of shock ran through Roy. Meanwhile, Richard, now Chief of Operations for Afghanistan, mobilized his network of assets, a silent web stretching across the country, tasked with locating the abducted journalists with utmost urgency. Informers scrambled to contact their sources, their whispers cutting through the shadows. One, embedded deep within the treacherous Tora Bora mountain range, delivered the crucial intelligence to Richard.

"Sir, the four reporters are being held in a cave in Tora Bora. They are hostages at one of Al-Qaeda's hidden bases. I'm sending you the exact coordinates. The base is guarded by 15 highly trained terrorists."

Tora Bora and the surrounding Safed Koh range, a labyrinth of natural caverns carved by ancient streams into the limestone, provided a formidable sanctuary for the enemy. Richard immediately briefed CIA Headquarters in Langley, and the gravity of the situation reached the White House. The President's response was swift and unequivocal: "There will be no negotiations with these terrorists. Prepare a team to strike Tora Bora and extract those hostages immediately."

The responsibility for the entire operation fell squarely on Richard's shoulders. He meticulously gathered every scrap of intelligence, every minute detail from his network, his eyes dissecting the hostage site through the cold gaze of the live satellite feed. A plan began to form in his mind, a high-stakes gamble to snatch the hostages from Al-Qaeda's grasp. For this perilous mission, Richard chose SEAL Team 3. However, fate had dealt a cruel blow: Simon Smith, the team's steadfast leader, was side-lined, his leg broken in an unforeseen accident. Simon, with unwavering trust in Roy's capabilities, designated him as the temporary head for this critical operation. The mission would unfold under Roy's command, his and his team's extensive experience in the region their greatest asset. Richard knew Roy's record: successful operations executed flawlessly, with every member of his squad returning home.

Two days later, Roy received the call. Richard arrived at the base, his presence radiating urgency. Without preamble, he briefed Roy.

"Morning, Roy. You know the situation. You and your team need to rescue those hostages from the Tora Bora caves. The area is incredibly dangerous, geographically challenging. The caves are a maze of twists, turns, and multiple entry-exit points. You need to be extremely careful. Memorize the entire area before you move in. There are approximately 15 highly trained and well-equipped militants guarding the hostages. Every step must be precise, or those reporters' lives will be in grave danger."

"Yes, sir. My team and I will begin planning immediately," Roy affirmed, his voice resolute.

"Time is critical. The deadline is in three days. We need to strike before then."

"We'll do our best, sir," Roy replied, the weight of responsibility settling upon him.

Under Richard's guidance, Roy and his team plunged into the intricate task of planning the rescue. Roy pored over the live satellite feeds of the cave system, his mind constructing a detailed strategy.

"Rescuing the hostages is only half the battle," Roy thought, his gaze fixed on the satellite images. "The extraction will be even tougher. It's mountainous terrain; an airlift from the site is impossible. We'll have to get out on foot."

Twelve grueling hours later, Roy had a plan. He presented it to Simon Smith, seeking the seasoned leader's critical eye. Simon, despite his injury, offered his insights and ultimately gave his approval. Roy then briefed Richard.

"Richard, this is the plan. In my estimation, the operation will take approximately 45 minutes. We'll need an airlift arranged seven miles from the hostage site. And one more thing: once the rescue is complete, at my command, I need a drone ready for a missile strike on the cave entrance, eliminating any chance of retaliation."

"Hmm, the plan seems sound," Richard mused, his mind racing. "Let me brief Langley and the White House. You'll have confirmation within 12 hours."

Richard presented the mission to Langley and the White House. The green light was given. The operation had to proceed within the next 12 hours. Richard immediately informed Roy. Roy gathered his 15-member team.

"Good morning, boys," Roy began, his voice calm but firm. "The operation to rescue the hostages will commence in exactly 11 hours. We'll have a five-mile trek to the hostage point. After the rescue, we need to move fast. A drone strike is scheduled for the cave entrance exactly one hour and 45 minutes after we initiate the mission. There are approximately 10 to 15 militants guarding the caves, the exact number is uncertain. Everyone, memorize the map of the area and the specific cave where the hostages are being held. Any questions?"

"No, sir," the team responded in unison.

"Okay, dismissed," Roy commanded.

Two hours before the strike, Roy ordered his team to prepare. A palpable tension filled the air. The terrain was unfamiliar, a treacherous labyrinth of caves and mountains, but their training and unwavering confidence held them steady.

The time arrived. The team, fully equipped and ready, boarded the waiting choppers. They were flown to the Safed Koh range, near the Tora Bora caves, and dropped five miles from their objective. Roy gathered his team.

"Boys, this is a dangerous area. Keep your eyes peeled, stay alert. The enemy could be anywhere. It's mountainous, so watch your footing."

Their journey towards the hostage point began, a slow and arduous climb through the rocky terrain. Every step was a calculated risk, a potential for injury and lost time. Around noon, with two miles still to cover, they paused for a brief reconnaissance. One teammate deployed a small, silent drone, sending it ahead towards the cave entrance. The feed revealed five armed men guarding the opening. After analyzing their positions, the team began their final approach. They reached the area, taking cover behind large rocks. Three snipers positioned themselves on a high vantage point, while the rest of the team, divided into Alpha (Roy's group), Charlie, Bravo, and Echo, took positions behind the rocks. Their weapons were fitted with silencers, ensuring a stealthy entry.

"Delta team, in position," the snipers reported.

"Alpha team, in position."

"Charlie team, in position."

"Bravo team, in position."

"Echo team, in position."

"Delta team, targets locked?" Roy queried.

"Yes, sir."

"Engage and shoot."

Five muffled shots echoed through the mountains.

"Targets neutralized, sir."

"I'm taking point, heading towards the cave," Roy commanded. "Charlie, Bravo, and Echo, follow us. Delta team, secure the entrance, watch for intruders."

Roy and his team moved into the darkness of the cave. He spotted a militant cleaning his weapon, aimed, and fired, dragging the body aside. Charlie team took the lead. The cave's interior was dimly lit by a few generator-powered lights. Charlie team veered left, while Alpha and Echo teams took the right path. Charlie team discovered a small chamber where three militants were sleeping. They moved silently, but a misplaced footstep on a discarded glass shard shattered the stillness. One militant's eyes snapped open, seeing the intruders. Before he could reach for his weapon, Charlie team eliminated all three.

"Three men neutralized," Charlie team reported.

Alpha and Echo teams approached a heavy iron door, two guards standing watch. Echo team, concealed behind a rocky outcrop, took aim and neutralized the two militants. Peeking through the doorway, they saw four hostages lying on the ground, their hands cuffed. Echo team prepared a breaching charge. Meanwhile, Alpha team continued further, taking a right turn, and found three more militants guarding another room. Alpha team swiftly took them down. Roy approached the door the three militants had been guarding and knocked. As soon as the door creaked open, Roy fired, killing the man inside – the leader of the 14-militant guard.

Echo team detonated the breaching charge, the iron door crashing to the ground. They secured the four hostages and began moving towards the exit. As they emerged, Delta team's urgent voice crackled over the comms.

"15 more armed men are entering the cave! We managed to take out six, nine are inside! Beware!"

"How the hell did they know we were here?" Roy exclaimed, his mind racing. "We only have 12 minutes to get out! Charlie, Echo, and Bravo, take defensive positions!"

As they moved towards the exit, gunfire erupted around them. The teams took cover, positioning the hostages behind them. A Bravo team member hurled two grenades in quick succession, eliminating three militants. Echo team provided cover fire while Alpha and Charlie teams advanced slowly, aiming and firing at the remaining six militants. They took down five. Suddenly, an armed militant emerged from a side passage, firing wildly, hitting Eric, Roy's closest friend, hard. Blood soaked Eric's hand, rendering it useless. Roy instantly aimed and shot the militant dead.

Five minutes remained until the evacuation and the drone strike. Two Bravo team members administered first aid to Eric, helping him move towards the exit. All teams, along with the freed hostages, emerged from the cave and moved towards the designated safe zone.

"Everyone run! The missile is dropping in two minutes!" Roy yelled.

The moment they reached the safe zone, a deafening BOOM echoed through the mountains, and the entire cave system vanished in a cloud of dust and debris. After a brief moment, they began the arduous seven-mile trek towards the airlift point. Exhaustion gnawed at them, their progress slow due to the tired hostages and the injured Eric. Thirst became another enemy, their water bag lost in the earlier firefight. Driven by Roy's relentless encouragement, they finally neared their objective.

A message crackled over Roy's radio.

"Ride arrived."

"Almost there," Roy replied, his voice hoarse.

Two choppers materialized in the distance. Four men emerged, rushing to assist. They immediately attended to Eric, providing urgent medical care. One by one, the team and the hostages boarded the choppers. The choppers lifted off, and within an hour, they landed back at Bagram Base. Eric was immediately transported to the hospital. Richard met Roy, his face etched with relief and admiration. He clapped Roy on the shoulder.

"Congratulations, Roy. Another successful mission."

The rescued reporters were also taken for medical attention. Operation TORA BORA was complete.

Chapter 9: Finding the Mole.

The weight of the Tora Bora operation settled heavily on Roy's mind the next day. A nagging question persisted, a shadow of doubt in the victory.

"Who could have leaked our intel to Al-Qaeda? There's a mole, I know it. I have to find them."

He placed a call to Richard in Langley, his voice edged with urgency.

"Hello, Richard."

"Hello, Roy. What can I do for you?"

"You know how those extra fifteen men attacked us during the mission? I need to know how they got wind of our strike. Someone inside is feeding them information, I'm sure of it. Will you help me find this mole? If we don't root them out now, every future mission will be compromised."

"Yeah, you're right, Roy. This is serious. I'll definitely help you. What resources do you need?"

"I need to know exactly how many people on your end knew the precise date and time of the mission. I'll gather the same from my team. Then, let's cross-reference their call records and financials. I'm betting we'll find a lead there."

"That's a solid plan. Meet me at my office on Monday at 11:00 AM," Richard agreed, his tone grim.

Roy pulled his own connections, reaching out to a trusted associate high up in the Navy SEAL hierarchy. This contact discreetly provided him with a list of individuals who had access to the mission's sensitive details, including his own team members. By Monday morning, Roy was en route to Langley, the CIA headquarters, his mind a whirlwind of suspicion and determination.

"Good morning, Roy. Did you bring the list?" Richard greeted him, his eyes sharp.

"Yes, I have it right here," Roy replied, handing over the document.

"Give it to me. I'll have my agents pull their information. I've already compiled the data on everyone on my end. Let's see what we can find."

"Let's do it."

"Coffee?"

"Yeah, please. I could use it."

As they sipped their coffee, a tense silence filled the room. They began meticulously scrutinizing the information Richard had gathered, cross-referencing phone logs from the week leading up to the mission with financial transactions during the same period. Six hours crawled by, each dead end adding to the frustration. Finally, one of Richard's colleagues entered, handing him a file containing the information on the individuals Roy had flagged.

"It's here. Let's check it quickly. Hopefully, we'll find something."

"Yeah, fingers crossed. Otherwise, we're back to square one."

They resumed their painstaking analysis, sifting through phone records and financial statements. Eighteen names from Roy's list yielded nothing. Roy picked up the file for the nineteenth name.

"Simon's phone and financial records," he said, a reluctant tone in his voice. "I'm sure there won't be anything, but we have to be thorough."

"Absolutely. No stone unturned."

Roy began reviewing Simon's financial history. A large, anomalous transfer caught his eye.

"Holy moly! $250,000, three days before the mission!" Roy exclaimed, his eyes wide with disbelief. "Richard, can you pull Simon's call records from three days before the mission?"

"Yeah, hold on."

Richard accessed the records, his expression shifting from focused to surprised. A series of calls, seven times within a single hour, all to the same unknown number.

"Roy, there are multiple calls to this number, seven times in one hour. I'll have my agent trace it immediately."

"Yeah, please do it fast."

A wave of disbelief washed over Roy. His own team leader, a man he respected, potentially a traitor.

"Simon… behind this? I still can't believe it."

"It's shocking, I agree. Let's wait for the trace on that number."

Moments later, Richard's assistant, Mike, rushed in with the information.

"Sir, we traced the number. It's a burner phone originating from Kabul, Afghanistan."

"Can we pinpoint its exact location?" Richard pressed.

"Yeah, let me check," Mike replied, quickly accessing the data. He pinpointed the location using the nearest cell phone tower. "Got it."

"Call our Kabul asset immediately. Arrest the individual using that phone number and bring him in for interrogation at our safe house," Richard ordered, his voice hardening.

Within the hour, Richard's asset in Kabul apprehended the suspect. After two tense hours of interrogation, the truth began to unravel.

"Sir, he confessed to transferring $250,000 into Simon Smith's account. He claims his commander ordered the transfer," the Kabul agent reported over the phone.

"So, it's confirmed. Simon is the mole." Richard's voice was grim.

"I can't believe this," Roy muttered, a sense of betrayal washing over him. "I trusted that guy. He betrayed us, the whole country. What do we do now, Richard?"

"We have to arrest him, Roy. Send a team to Bagram Base. Simon's still at the hospital, recovering from his 'accident.' Doctors were planning to discharge him today."

"Orders sent," Mike confirmed quickly.

Thirty minutes later, Roy received a call from Eric, still recovering in the same hospital.

"Military police just came to arrest Simon, but he's gone. He left about fifteen minutes before they arrived. What's going on, Roy?"

"Damn it, he's on the run! Did he say where he was going?"

"No, just that he had something he needed to take care of."

"Okay, no problem. You just focus on getting better. I'll fill you in when we meet. Bye."

Roy hung up and immediately informed Richard about Simon's escape.

"Simon vanished before the MPs could take him into custody."

"Shit! Mike, track his cell phone!"

"Found it, sir. He's at Kabul International Airport."

"Alert airport security. Detain him!"

"Done, sir."

Simon was apprehended at the airport, his attempt to flee to Mexico thwarted. Military Police took him into custody, preparing for his extradition back to the U.S. to face the consequences of his treachery.

Roy let out a long breath, a sense of grim satisfaction washing over him.

"Thank you, Richard, for letting me help find the mole."

"No, thank you, Roy. You did excellent work uncovering this. I must say, you should consider a transfer to the CIA. You'd be a valuable asset."

"Thank you for the offer. I'll definitely consider it in the future, but right now, my place is leading my SEAL team."

They exchanged a final goodbye and returned to their respective duties, the weight of the betrayal still lingering in the air.

Six months later, Richard's team intercepted another disturbing chatter among a suspected terrorist group. This time, the threat originated not from Afghanistan, but from Iran. The criminal organization, known as SCRIOS, was led by the notorious Bashir Hashemi, a dangerous figure wanted by numerous countries. The intercepted communication came from Rashid Mazdani, Bashir's right-hand man. The CIA had been tracking Mazdani for two years without success, but this time, the chatter hinted at a significant terrorist plot targeting the United States. Richard received immediate orders from his superiors: assemble a team of experts and neutralize the threat before it spiraled out of control. Jack Murphy, the head of the CIA, summoned Richard for an urgent meeting. Richard knocked on his office door.

"May I come in, sir?"

"Yes, Richard, have a seat."

"What are your orders, sir?"

"Richard, this terrorist threat is critical. I have direct orders from D.C. to make this our top priority. Organize a team of our best agents to work on this mission. You'll have access to all necessary resources, no questions asked. I want this threat neutralized, and I want daily updates."

"Understood, sir. I'll do my best."

Richard returned to his office, his mind already assembling the pieces of the puzzle, recruiting the best minds for this new, high-stakes mission.

"Mike, give me a list of our top candidates for this. I need a male operative, smart and an expert in combat. A female agent, beautiful yet lethal, capable of luring our target and extracting information. Someone with deep connections who can arrange any transportation and weapon needs. And our best hacker, someone who can crack any system."

"Okay, sir. Give me a few hours. I'll compile some names."

Richard sat, his mind racing through potential candidates. Suddenly, one name surfaced: Roy Spectre, the head of NAVY SEAL Team 3. Richard had worked with him on two previous missions and knew his sharp intellect and decisive action. He decided to recommend Roy to Jack Murphy. Soon after, Mike returned with the list.

"Sir, here's a list of twenty top candidates, with a brief description of their specialties."

"Give me some time to sort this according to their skills."

"Okay, sir."

Richard narrowed down the list. His choices were: Roy Spectre – Smart and Combat Specialist; Sofia Russo – Beautiful & Lethal; Max Ricci – Badass Hacker; and John Edward – Weapons, transportation, and explosives specialist, a man of formidable size.

Sofia Russo was a legendary independent contractor, her beauty as striking as her combat skills were deadly. A brunette with piercing green eyes, standing at an imposing 5'11", she possessed an uncanny ability to lure any target with her allure, then eliminate the threat with cold precision. Governments around the world called upon her when vital information needed extraction or dangerous criminals needed silencing.

Max Ricci, a computer prodigy, was the ultimate hacker. A wiry 5'7" tech genius, he had famously hacked the Federal Reserve System at the age of fourteen. Now, he used his extraordinary skills ethically, working independently for various U.S. government institutions.

John Edward was a mountain of a man, towering at 6'3" and weighing a solid 260 pounds of muscle. An expert in explosives, he had a global network of contacts who could procure any weapon, material, or transportation needed, anywhere in the world. His deep connections within various intelligence agencies were unparalleled.

Richard took the refined list to Jack Murphy.

"The team is ready, sir."

"Show me… Hmm, who is this Roy Spectre?"

"Sir, I specifically want Roy Spectre. He's brilliant and capable of handling this type of mission quickly and efficiently. He's currently the head of NAVY SEAL Team 3. I request his transfer to this team."

"No problem, consider it done. This is a matter of national security. What about the others – Sofia, Max, and John?"

"Sir, they are the best in their respective fields. Together, with proper training and guidance, this team will undoubtedly accomplish the mission."

"Start getting the team ready. Meanwhile, let me speak with the Head of the Department of Defence, Riley Maxwell, regarding Roy Spectre's transfer."

Jack contacted the DOD head, emphasizing the critical need for Roy Spectre on this mission. The DOD head immediately agreed and called Roy directly.

"Roy, Riley here."

"Good morning, sir."

"Good morning. The CIA needs you for an important mission. You have four days. Pack your things. You're being transferred to the CIA. Report to Richard on Tuesday morning at 8:00 AM."

"Understood, sir. I'll contact Richard on Tuesday."

"Good. Make your country proud, son. Goodbye."

"For sure, sir. Goodbye."

Roy packed his belongings and informed his team.

"Guys, I have some important news. I received orders from Sir Riley. I'm being permanently transferred to the CIA. It's been an honor working with you all. Thank you for your support."

His teammates applauded, offering hugs and congratulations. Eric, though happy for Roy, felt a pang of sadness at his friend's departure.

"Congratulations, bro! I'm really happy for you. Call me if you need anything."

"Thanks, brother. I will. And hey, take care. I recommended you as the future head of this team."

"Thanks, man."

They embraced, a silent farewell between brothers-in-arms. Roy decided to make a quick trip to New York to see his mother and gather some personal items before starting his new chapter with the CIA. He took a late-night flight, planning to surprise Veronica. He arrived at his luxurious penthouse at 7:00 AM and knocked on the door.

"Who could that be so early?" Veronica exclaimed, opening the door to find her son standing before her.

"Roy! Son, what a wonderful surprise!"

She embraced him tightly, tears of joy streaming down their faces. They went inside, Roy setting down his luggage in the living room and sinking comfortably onto the couch.

"How are you, Mom? It's so good to be home after so long. It feels amazing."

"I'm well, Roy, so thrilled to see you. How many days will you be staying?"

"Hmm, sorry, Mom. I'll have to leave the day after tomorrow. I've been transferred to the CIA and need to report on Tuesday at 8:00 AM."

"What! The CIA? From the Navy SEALs?"

"I don't know the specifics. They need me for a mission. I got the call yesterday."

"Okay, but you just arrived, and you're leaving again so soon? Roy, take some time off, spend some time with your mother."

"I know, Mom, it's been too long. But what can I do? I have my orders. Don't worry, I'll come back for a longer visit next time."

"Alright, son. Now go take a bath and get ready. I'll make you a nice breakfast."

"Okay, Mom."

Roy went to his room, unpacked his bag, and lay down on his bed, a wave of nostalgia and peace washing over him. The warmth and familiarity of his childhood room brought back cherished memories. Soon, he freshened up and joined his mother for breakfast.

"Wow, Mom, my favourite – pancakes!"

"Yes, I made your favourite."

"They're delicious. I missed this so much out in the field."

Two days passed quickly. It was time for Roy to report to Langley. As he packed his bag, his eyes fell upon the toy robot his father had given him before he died. Tears welled up as he picked it up, memories of his father flooding his mind. He carefully placed the toy in his bag and said goodbye to his mother.

"Goodbye, Mom. Take care. See you soon. I'll call you as soon as I land."

"Goodbye, son. Be careful."

They hugged, and Roy stepped into his new life. Early morning at 4:00 AM, he headed to the airport for his flight to Langley, Virginia. His flight was on time, and he landed as scheduled. A car from the CIA was waiting to take him to the office in Langley. As he reached the main gate, he paused for a moment, a sense of anticipation and the weight of the unknown settling upon him.

"Hmm, welcome to the new life, Roy."

Chapter 10: Welcome to The CIA.

A new chapter unfurled in Roy's life, the enigmatic world of the CIA beckoning.

He found Richard in his office, the air buzzing with unspoken possibilities.

"Hello, Richard."

"Roy! Welcome to the CIA. It's great to finally have you here," Richard greeted him warmly, a hint of a knowing smile playing on his lips.

"So, you finally lured me to the dark side," Roy quipped, a touch of amusement in his voice.

"You were always destined for this path, Roy."

"Feels good to be here," Roy admitted, a sense of anticipation stirring within him.

"As you know, Mike will show you to your temporary quarters. Take today to settle in. Tomorrow, I'll introduce you to your new team. We'll then begin mission-specific training, preparing you for any threat you might encounter. Being a spy is about accessing information, and to do that, we must become like water, blending seamlessly with our surroundings to extract what we need. Sometimes, things won't go according to plan, so we must be ready for anything. This training will amplify your already impressive skills. Good luck with it."

"Understood. Thank you. I'm looking forward to the training. Happy to be here. See you tomorrow."

True to his word, Roy met Richard the next morning. Richard led him to a conference room where three other individuals awaited their new leader. Richard's introduction was concise and impactful.

"Everyone, meet Roy Spectre. Former Head of NAVY SEAL Team 3, and now, he will be leading your team."

A chorus of "Hi" and welcoming nods greeted Roy. Richard then introduced him to Sofia, Max, and John.

"Roy, this is Sofia Russo – beautiful and lethal. Meet Max Ricci – our expert hacker. And this is John Edward – combat, explosives, and transportation specialist."

"Hello, it's a pleasure to meet you all," Roy said, extending a hand to each of them.

"You'll all be heading out today for 30 days of intensive training tailored for this specific mission," Richard explained. "You'll learn new combat styles, master advanced tech gear, and hone crucial spy tactics. Mike will take you from here."

Mike led them away from the polished corridors of the CIA headquarters. The training facility, when they arrived, was a stark contrast: an old, dilapidated warehouse with broken windows, rust-streaked walls, and an eerie silence hanging in the deserted neighbourhood. It was the perfect, inconspicuous location for clandestine training.

Mike drove the car into the warehouse's underground parking. Stepping out, they exchanged curious glances, trying to decipher the entrance to the actual facility. Mike guided them towards a rusty old door. Beside it, a small, equally corroded iron box sat innocuously. Mike opened the box, revealing a sleek, modern smart access lock. He entered a code, then placed his finger on the scanner. With a soft click, the rusty door creaked open, revealing not the expected dusty interior, but the gleaming entrance of an elevator.

"Whoa! That's… interesting," Roy commented, a hint of a smile playing on his lips.

They all stepped into the elevator. Mike swiped his RFID card, and the elevator smoothly descended. Ten floors below, the doors opened to reveal an ultra-modern facility. A vast hall buzzed with activity, agents moving with purpose between sleek desks and glass-walled offices. Mike led them to a research room, a haven of cutting-edge spy technology being tested and refined.

"Wow, this is amazing! Hey Max, look at that suit they're testing," Roy exclaimed, his eyes wide with fascination.

"Dude, nothing's happening to it! They're trying to burn it, hit it, even shoot it!" Max replied, equally impressed.

As they watched the seemingly indestructible suit, a lead scientist, Mark Hendriks, approached Mike and the new team.

"Hello Mark, meet our new recruits: Roy, Sofia, Max, and John," Mike introduced.

"Welcome, everyone. The suit you're observing is next-gen advanced combat gear," Mark explained, his eyes gleaming with pride. "It amplifies the wearer's strength significantly. It's 100% bulletproof and can withstand considerable blasts. It will increase your physical capabilities by 100%. It's still in trials, but it should be ready by next month."

"That's incredible, Mark! I hope I get a chance to test it. That would be fun," Roy said, a thrill of excitement in his voice.

"Roy, this isn't a toy; it needs to be handled with extreme care," Mark cautioned, a hint of a smile softening his stern expression.

"Understood."

They were then introduced to their training officer, Carl Cuban.

"Carl, meet your new students. You have thirty days to make them ready," Mike stated.

"Thirty days? This isn't some assembly line where finished agents pop out at the other end! They need rigorous training, every vulnerability eradicated. How can I possibly prepare them in thirty days? And are *they* even capable of it?" Carl grumbled, scepticism etched on his face.

"Sir, just so you know, I'm ex-Navy SEAL," Roy interjected calmly. "We've been through some pretty intense training. This shouldn't be too difficult."

"This isn't the Navy SEALs, son," Carl retorted, his gaze sharp. "Being an agent means being the smartest person in the room. You'll need to master information extraction, the art of persuasion. You'll be operating among the wealthy, possibly billionaires – the very enemies we'll be facing. Without proper training, you'll be exposed in seconds. You'll need to learn to blend in like water, and much, much more."

"Okay, sir. We'll do our best," Roy replied, his determination unwavering.

"Anyway, Mike, would you please show them to their quarters?" Carl sighed, a hint of resignation in his voice.

"Sure."

Mike escorted them to their rooms.

"Get some rest," he advised. "Because starting tomorrow, you won't be getting much for the next thirty days."

They settled into their rooms, a mix of anticipation and apprehension swirling within them, and enjoyed their last few hours of relative peace.

The next day, the rigorous training began. Combat was the first order of business.

"First, we'll master advanced combat skills – a form of Mixed Martial Arts," Carl announced. "You'll be trained to face any powerful human threat, increasing your speed and efficiency in a fight."

Their training commenced with intense physical conditioning and combat drills. Alongside the physical aspects, they received crucial instruction on behaviour, appropriate attire, and the subtle art of conversation aimed at extracting information. Roy excelled in the human behaviour training, his prior experience giving him a significant advantage. They were taught advanced driving techniques, including high-speed manoeuvres and evasive tactics. They even learned to pilot helicopters and small planes, skills that might prove vital in the field. They were being meticulously moulded into perfect agents.

The training was relentless, stretching to eighteen hours each day. Roy, accustomed to the gruelling schedules of the Navy SEALs, adapted relatively easily. Twenty days flew by, their skills sharpening with each passing hour. One evening, during a rare moment of respite at dinner, Sofia turned to Roy.

"Roy, you're doing incredibly well in everything, especially combat."

"Thanks," Roy replied. "During Navy SEAL training, we were pushed to our limits in combat scenarios. The only real difference here is the focus on advanced MMA."

"I still don't understand why *I* need such intense physical training," Max grumbled. "I'll be spending most of my time behind a computer."

"You won't always be behind a computer, Max," John countered. "What if someone attacks you? We won't always be there to protect you. This training will help you survive those situations. Besides, we might need you as a decoy sometimes."

"Ha-ha. Very funny," Max retorted dryly.

"Alright, guys, let's finish dinner quickly. I'm exhausted and need some sleep," Roy said, stifling a yawn.

"Likewise," Sofia agreed.

They retreated to their rooms, their bodies aching but their minds buzzing with newfound skills.

Ten more days of relentless training forged them into a cohesive unit, ready to face any challenge.

"Alright, team, well done," Carl announced, a rare hint of pride in his voice. "You've made remarkable progress. I can confidently say you're ready for anything. Remember, in the field, you need to have each other's backs. That's the only way you'll succeed. Now, it's time for the real mission. Mike will pick you up in three hours. Pack your bags."

"Thank you, sir. It was an honor to train under you," Roy said, extending his hand.

"Thank you, sir," Sofia echoed.

"Thank you, sir," Max added.

"Thank you, sir," John concluded.

They each shook Carl's hand, a silent acknowledgment of the gruelling but transformative training. Mike arrived promptly.

"So, how was the training, guys?"

"Tiring, but we learned a lot," Roy replied, a hint of a smile.

"Yeah, Mike, incredibly tiring. Eighteen-hour days," Sofia added, rolling her eyes playfully.

"You know, Mike, now no one can mess with this computer nerd. I can actually fight now!" Max declared, puffing out his chest.

"What about you, John?" Mike chuckled.

"Yo, it was good. Now I can fly any plane or chopper. No more hiring pilots for my… transportation needs."

"Great. Richard's waiting for you all back at headquarters. He wants to brief you on the mission."

Finally, they were trained, equipped, and ready. The real test was about to begin.

Roy, Sofia, Max, and John found Richard waiting for them in his office.

"Welcome back, everyone. How was your training?" Richard asked, his gaze sweeping over them.

"It was intense, Richard. But I think we're ready," Roy stated confidently.

"Yes, we are," Sofia echoed, a determined glint in her eyes.

"Good. Let's head to the conference room. I'll brief you on the mission."

They followed Richard to the conference room, where Mike was already waiting.

"Have a seat, everyone. As you can see on the screen, this is Bashir Hashemi, the leader of SCRIOS – a major crime syndicate in Iran. He commands a large army of loyal militants. Last month, we intercepted chatter from his right-hand man, Rashid Mazdani, hinting at a massive attack on US soil. Our first objective is to abduct his accountant, Hasan Azhar, to extract information about this planned attack. He's currently in Paris, France. He handles all of Bashir's finances and Hawala operations. We have intel suggesting he'll be meeting someone regarding a deal in three days at Hotel Loisir. We're all leaving for Paris tomorrow morning. Mike will take you to Mark Hendriks. I believe you've met him? He'll provide you with all the necessary gadgets for this mission."

"Okay! We're ready to rumble," Roy declared, a surge of adrenaline coursing through him.

"Yes, let's do it," Sofia added, her voice laced with anticipation.

Mike led them back to Mark's lab, a treasure trove of clandestine technology.

"Ah, there you are! Richard called and told me to equip you all. Wait here, your gear will be ready shortly."

Mark directed his team, and an array of sophisticated gadgets was laid out before them.

"This is a handgun, but not just any handgun," Mark began, holding up a sleek weapon. "It has a built-in screen and camera. Lock onto your target, and the smart bullet will track it, ensuring you never miss. The bullet is powerful enough to penetrate bulletproof glass, metal, and Kevlar. Here are four – one for each of you."

"Hmm, wow! That's incredible, Mark. Can I test it somewhere?" Roy asked, his curiosity piqued.

"Sure. See that dummy over there? It's designed to move erratically. Just lock on and see the result."

Roy targeted the dummy, the screen on the handgun glowing red as it acquired the lock. He fired, and the bullet unerringly struck the moving target.

"Now *that's* what I call a smart gun," John chuckled, impressed.

"This spray bottle contains a bulletproof liquid," Mark continued. "Spray it all over your body; it will absorb into your skin, creating a temporary bulletproof shield. One application lasts for seven days."

"Whoa! That's new. Never seen anything like it," Sofia remarked, her eyes widening.

"Take a look at this cell phone, Max. You'll love it. Our best engineers designed this. We can track you even when it's switched off. It has a built-in system that can hack into any facility with a single click. It can unlock anything and bypass any security in seconds."

"That's awesome! You've just made my job a whole lot easier. Can't wait to try it!" Max exclaimed, his fingers itching to get hold of the device.

"This smartwatch has a tracker and a laser capable of cutting through any known metal. You can also use it to trigger small blasts. And this ring," Mark held up a seemingly ordinary ring, "just twist it and throw it at your target – it's a miniature explosive."

"Yo, the *blast* ring sounds fun," John grinned.

"We also have these smart lenses for you," Mark presented four pairs of sleek contact lenses. "These will overlay information directly into your vision – mission updates, facial recognition with real-time background checks, and a 500x optical zoom."

"Can we try them?" Roy asked.

"Sure, go ahead."

Roy inserted the lenses.

"Oh man, it shows everything, Mark! It says you have an advanced engineering degree from MIT. Max, it says you were born in Houston, Texas."

"Wait, Roy, we're not doing background checks here," Sofia interjected, a hint of amusement in her voice.

"Okay," Roy chuckled.

"Now, I've saved the best for last. This is the Power Serum, codenamed P30," Mark revealed a small vial filled with a shimmering liquid. "This serum will amplify all your physical abilities by 40% – your punches will be 40% stronger, your speed will increase. Mike will inject you with it before the mission. The effects last for a week."

"Yeah, I could definitely use some of that Serum," Max admitted, a touch of nervousness in his voice.

"This Serum also has a tracking device embedded within it. We'll be able to monitor your vitals and location."

"Mark, these gadgets are fantastic. Thanks," Roy said, genuinely impressed.

"You're welcome. Just try to use them responsibly," Mark replied, a wry smile on his face.

They were then dismissed to their rooms to rest before their early departure. Back in his room, Roy began packing.

"Better pack now; we have to leave early."

As he folded his clothes, his gaze fell upon the toy robot he had brought from his childhood home. He picked it up, a wave of nostalgia washing over him as he remembered his father. While fiddling with it, he heard a faint rattling sound. He detached the robot's head and shook it. A small object fell onto his bed. Roy picked it up, examining it closely.

"It looks like some kind of circuit… but how did it get inside the robot? And the robot still works. It's not part of it… Wait a minute! I remember this! The same thing came loose years ago when I was playing with it, right after the robbery… What if someone sent that robber to look for this thing at my place? Anyway, let me put this on my neck chain. Time to sleep. Early morning tomorrow."

He secured the small circuit onto his chain and drifted off to sleep. He woke up before dawn, got ready, and received a call from Mike.

"Car's coming to pick you up in ten minutes. Be ready."

The car arrived, and Roy joined Sofia, Max, and John, who were already inside. They were driven to the airport, where Richard and Mike waited beside a sleek CIA private jet. The Gulfstream G500 gleamed under the pre-dawn light. They boarded, the luxurious interior taking their breath away.

"Finally, flying private!" Max exclaimed, his eyes wide with delight.

"Hello, everyone. Ready for our first mission?" Richard asked, a hint of excitement in his voice.

"Born ready," Roy replied, a surge of anticipation coursing through him.

"Fasten your seat belts. We're taking off now."

Chapter 11: The Accomplice.

The Parisian evening painted the sky in hues of grey as their aircraft touched down at 4:00 PM. A pair of imposing, black-tinted Mercedes-Benz G-Wagons idled near the aircraft, their presence a silent testament to the urgency of their mission. As they disembarked, a noticeable chill permeated the air.

Roy and Max both shivered, pulling their collars higher.

"Man, it's cold out here," Roy commented, his breath misting slightly.

"Yeah, the temperature's showing 48°F," Max replied, adjusting his jacket. "Only a couple of degrees colder than D.C., but it's pretty windy, so it feels closer to 37°F."

Richard was greeted by Anton Berger, the CIA Station Chief in Paris, who had personally come to assist them. Whispers from Langley had underscored the mission's critical importance. Richard introduced his team.

"Hey, Anton, good to finally meet you. Heard great things about you in Langley. This is my team: Roy, Sofia, Max, and John. And this is Mike, my indispensable assistant."

"Welcome to Paris, the City of Love, everyone," Anton said, extending a hand to each of them. "Get in the cars; let's head to the hotel first."

As they drove through the elegant Parisian streets, Roy pointed out a familiar landmark.

"Hey, look! The Eiffel Tower. Still as beautiful as I remember."

"You've been here before?" Sofia asked, her gaze following his.

"Yeah, a few years back. Came with my mom for a holiday when I was in university."

"Oh, great," Sofia replied.

"This is my first time," Max chimed in, his eyes wide with wonder. "It's lovely. I already know what souvenir I'm taking back home."

"What souvenir?" John inquired, raising an eyebrow.

Max stretched his arm out with a cheesy grin. "A French kiss."

"Oh yeah? Good luck with that," John smirked.

They soon arrived at their hotel, The Luxe Continental.

"Here we are," Anton announced. "The agency has booked six suites for you all. Freshen up, and at 6:00 PM sharp, an agency vehicle will escort you to our station. *Au revoir*."

"*À bientôt*," Richard replied.

They checked in and were shown to their respective rooms. As the bellboy opened the door to Max's suite, his jaw dropped.

"Wow! It's magnificent! A huge hall with a comfy couch, a minibar... look at that bed! And let me check out the bathroom... Whoa! It's massive! And a million-dollar view of the Eiffel Tower!"

"Hmm, nice room for a mission," Roy mused, already feeling the familiar focus settling in. "Let's shower first and then get ready. I'm starving. Maybe we can order some room service in the meantime."

Roy refreshed himself and satisfied his hunger with a quick meal. By six o'clock, they were all ready to head to the station.

Meeting in the hotel corridor, they descended to the waiting cars. The drive to the CIA's Paris Station was short. They were led into a sophisticated corporate building. Inside the elevator, their escort pressed the button for the 30th floor. Upon reaching their destination, a sign reading "A.I.C. Oil Corporation" hung above the entrance. A receptionist sat calmly at the front desk. Passing through the first door, they encountered a guarded second door. The escort swiped his card, and the door opened, revealing the true nature of "A.I.C. Oil Corporation." Around twenty-five people worked in the bustling station, surrounded by world-class tracking equipment. Anton stood in the center, overseeing agents monitoring a large screen displaying various feeds. He spotted Richard.

"Welcome, Richard, and team. Please, have a seat here. I'll brief you on the mission scheduled for the day after tomorrow in a few minutes."

They settled down to wait. Roy leaned towards Richard.

"Sir, do we have any intel on the weapon they're planning to use for the attack?"

"Not yet confirmed," Richard replied, his expression serious. "The meeting day after tomorrow is believed to be the finalization of the weapon deal. We'll likely know more then."

Anton approached them, ready to begin the briefing.

"Alright, as you all know, there's a meeting scheduled for the day after tomorrow at Hotel Loisir. Our assets have confirmed the time: 3:00 PM in the coffee lounge area. We have Hasan Azhar, the accountant, under surveillance. The plan is to abduct him three hours before the deal and turn him into our accomplice. Two of our operatives are currently at Hasan's residence, where his wife is staying. We will stage a fake attack and show Hasan a live feed of his wife in our custody. We'll threaten her life if he doesn't cooperate. Once he's compliant, we'll have him wear a wire. Roy and Sofia, you'll be waiting for them in the coffee lounge. Max and John will be in the van, monitoring the meeting. As soon as the other party arrives, Roy and Sofia will immediately abduct both of them and bring them to our safe house. After that, Roy, your priority will be extracting information about the weapon from the other individual."

"The idea seems excellent," Roy affirmed, his mind already strategizing.

"Now, all of you get back to the hotel and rest until tomorrow. Recharge for the mission. But listen carefully: we *must* extract this information. This is our last and best chance."

"Don't worry, Anton," Richard reassured him. "This is our most exceptional team. They're trained to handle anything."

Back at the hotel, John's stomach rumbled.

"Yo, I'm starving. Let's eat first."

"Yes, Richard, let's grab some food," Max echoed.

They headed to the hotel restaurant.

"Table for six, please," Mike requested the concierge.

They were seated and given the menus.

"The items listed in French sound incredibly delicious," Max commented, attempting a few pronunciations with a comical accent.

"Let's just order quickly, guys," Sofia replied, already scanning the options.

They ordered an array of exquisite dishes, accompanied by a bottle of fine wine. After dinner, while the others showed signs of fatigue, Roy seemed to have other plans.

"Guys, you go ahead. I'm going out for a walk. Sofia, would you like to join me?"

"I'd love to," she replied, a subtle warmth in her tone.

They strolled through the enchanting streets of Paris, admiring the city's architecture and soaking in the vibrant culture, their steps leading them towards the iconic Eiffel Tower. They stopped nearby, gazing up at the magnificent iron structure.

"What a spectacular view," Roy murmured, captivated.

"Indeed," Sofia agreed, her eyes reflecting the tower's lights.

"Have you been here before? Or is this your first time in Paris?" Roy asked.

"Nope, not my first time. I was here once for a mission, but I didn't have time to wander around like this. So, tell me, Roy, are you single, or is there someone special in your life?"

"No, I'm single," Roy replied. "I had a wonderful girlfriend back in university, but our paths diverged. That was a long time ago. Now, with our profession, there's not much time for relationships. And honestly, it's probably better to be unattached."

"Yeah, you're right. No commitments in our line of work. But I do need to blow off some steam sometimes," Sofia admitted, a playful glint in her eyes.

"Hmm, you're right," Roy echoed, a suggestive tone creeping into his voice. "Maybe I can help you with that tonight?"

"Well, not tonight," Sofia said, a slight blush rising on her cheeks. "Perhaps another time."

"I'll be waiting," Roy winked.

They walked back to the hotel in comfortable silence and retired to their separate rooms.

The day of the mission dawned. Roy, Sofia, Max, John, Mike, and Richard gathered at the station in the morning to prepare. Mike laid out the array of gadgets they had brought from headquarters.

"Alright, team, gear up. Let me spray you all with the bulletproof liquid."

"Mike, you won't be spraying me," Sofia declared with a playful smirk. "I'll get one of the female agents in the office to help."

"Oh, right. Of course," Mike stammered, slightly flustered.

"Remember, this spray will be effective for ten days," he reminded them.

Mike then produced the box containing the smartwatches, the Power Serum (P30), and the smart lenses.

"Now, Roy, Sofia, Max, and John, put on these watches and lenses. After that, I'll inject you with P30 – it'll give you a nice boost."

Mike administered the injections. After injecting Max, the hacker's eyes widened.

"Whoa! I feel powerful, man!"

"Max, it takes about an hour for the full effect," Mike chuckled.

"Well, even now, I feel strong!" Max insisted, flexing his arms.

"Good for you," John quipped.

"Now, everyone, put on these smart lenses," Mike instructed.

Roy, Sofia, Max, and John inserted the sleek lenses. Finally, Mike handed them their new cell phones and smart guns.

"Now I feel like a super-agent," Roy grinned, a familiar thrill coursing through him. "Feels good to be back in the game."

"Yo, let's kick some ass," John added, his energy palpable.

It was 11:00 AM. Anton's asset relayed information that Hasan was getting ready to leave his residence in fifteen minutes. Anton turned to Roy and Sofia.

"You two head over there immediately and abduct him."

"Yes, sir. On our way," Roy confirmed.

They rushed to the location where Hasan was staying.

"Sofia, let's hide in his car," Roy suggested. "When he comes out, we'll grab him at gunpoint."

"Good idea."

Using the advanced cell phone, which could bypass any vehicle's security system, they silently opened Hasan's car and concealed themselves in the back seat. Within minutes, Hasan emerged from his house, opened his car door, and settled into the driver's seat. As soon as he started the engine, Roy sat up, pressing his smart gun against the back of Hasan's head.

"Hands up! Do exactly as I say, or you die."

Roy instructed Sofia to check Hasan for any weapons. She found a handgun tucked under his jacket. They swiftly dragged him out of the car and bundled him into a waiting van, where two other agents covered his face with a black hood, disorienting him. Roy and Sofia drove away, taking Hasan to a secure safe house in Paris for interrogation. Meanwhile, Anton dispatched two of his men to Hasan's home to threaten his wife.

Roy and Sofia forced Hasan into a chair at an interrogation table, a harsh light glaring down on him. The room was stark, with cold iron walls and a heavy door.

"So, tell me, Hasan," Roy began, his voice calm but firm. "Who were you going to meet?"

"What are you talking about? I don't know you. Who are you?" Hasan stammered, his eyes darting nervously.

"Don't play coy with us, Hasan. We know everything about you. We know who you are, and we know you work for Bashir Hashemi."

"No, I don't know him! Who is Bashir? I run my own financial firm."

Roy slammed his hand on the table, the sudden noise making Hasan jump.

"Don't waste our time. We know you have a meeting at 3:00 PM at Hotel Loisir. Tell us what that deal is about."

"I… I don't know what you're talking about."

"It would be in your best interest to start talking, Hasan. Otherwise, there will be consequences."

"I already told you, I don't know!" Hasan insisted, his voice laced with fear.

"Show him the footage," Roy instructed Sofia.

Sofia turned on a television screen in the corner of the room, displaying a live feed of Hasan's wife, bound and terrified.

"Hasan, save me! They're going to kill me!" she cried out on the screen.

Hasan's face paled, his body trembling. Roy leaned closer, his voice low and menacing.

"Now, Hasan. Do you want your wife to live? Then tell me about the meeting."

"Please… please don't hurt my wife. I'll tell you anything you want to know."

"Tell me about this meeting. Who is the person you're meeting, and what's their name?"

"I… I don't know his name. I just got an order from Rashid to meet this man, make a payment, and receive the delivery of the weapon."

"Don't lie to me, Hasan! What's the name of the person, and what is the weapon? And how much are you supposed to pay?" Roy pressed, his patience wearing thin.

"I'm not lying! Why would I lie? You have my wife! I was told to pay one billion dollars into the seller's offshore account."

"One billion dollars! What kind of weapon is it, Hasan? Tell me!"

"I don't know! I've told you everything I know! Oh, and Rashid told me to give the man a codeword to identify him."

"What's the codeword?"

"WHITE LIES."

"Hasan," Roy said, his gaze intense. "It would be best for you and your wife if you do exactly as we say."

"What… what do I have to do?" Hasan pleaded, his eyes fixed on the screen showing his wife's distress.

"You're going to work with us. You'll go to that meeting and do exactly as you're told. Try anything clever, and your wife's life will be in grave danger. Do you understand?"

"Okay… okay. But please… please don't kill my wife."

"All I can say, Hasan, is that her life now depends entirely on you."

Chapter 12: Mr. X

The clock struck 2:00 PM, leaving a mere hour before Hasan's scheduled meeting. Roy and Sofia escorted a subdued Hasan to the black SUV, where two other agents waited. They parked a discreet distance from the Hotel Loisir, their vigil beginning.

Richard, accompanied by John and Max, positioned their heavily tinted Mercedes van, a mobile surveillance hub equipped with large screens and a sophisticated system, near the hotel. They arrived precisely on time.

Inside the van, Max initiated the hack into the hotel's surveillance network, the cafeteria's live feed materializing on their screens. Roy contacted Richard to confirm their positions.

"Richard, have you reached?"

"Yeah, I'm here with Max and John in the van. We're monitoring the cafeteria feed. What's your status?" Richard replied, his voice steady.

"We're in position in the car. Hasan's with us. I'll let you know as soon as we enter the hotel."

At 2:45 PM, the moment arrived. Roy and Sofia prepared to escort Hasan into the lion's den.

"We're entering the cafeteria," Roy radioed to Richard.

"Okay, roger that. We've got you on CCTV," Richard confirmed.

Roy and Sofia, with Hasan between them, entered the bustling cafeteria. Approximately ten tables were scattered around, six of them occupied. They spotted two empty tables near the exit and made their choice.

"Hasan, you sit at this table and don't look at us," Roy instructed, his voice low and firm. "We'll be at the table next to you. And one thing: we're watching you. Don't even think about trying anything smart. If we sense the slightest hesitation, you and your wife will both be dead."

"Okay… okay," Hasan mumbled, his eyes wide with fear.

Roy and Sofia settled at the adjacent table. "Sofia," Roy said, adopting a casual tone, "we'll act like you're my girlfriend."

A small smile flickered across Sofia's lips. "Very well."

Three o'clock arrived. Roy, Sofia, and the entire team held their breath, waiting for the mysterious contact. At 3:03 PM, a man in a cream suit and a wide-brimmed hat entered the cafeteria. He was around five-foot-ten, sporting a dense white beard and aviator sunglasses. His gaze swept the room, searching. Hasan subtly whispered, "WHITE LIES." The man's eyes locked onto Hasan, confirming he had found his contact. Two burly bodyguards accompanied him, but he gestured for them to remain outside the cafeteria. Richard watched the scene unfold on the surveillance feed. The man sat down with Hasan and inquired, "So, what is your name?"

"My name is Hasan. And yours, sir?"

"You can call me Mr. X."

"Have you brought the weapon?" Hasan asked, his voice barely above a whisper.

"Yes, it's with me. As soon as you transfer half the agreed amount, I'll show it to you."

Meanwhile, Roy and Sofia played their roles convincingly.

"You know, Sofia," Roy said, his arm casually draped over her chair, "you look even more beautiful today than the last time we met before I went abroad for work."

"Thanks, Roy," Sofia replied, leaning in slightly. "By the way, can we go back to my place after we have our coffee?"

"Sure!" Roy responded a little too enthusiastically, his eyes momentarily flicking towards Mr. X.

While feigning their romantic exchange, Roy discreetly activated his smart lens, focusing on Mr. X's face. The lens scanned his features, but the display returned: "No record found."

Hasan then spoke to Mr. X, his voice still hushed. "I'll pay half as soon as you show me the weapon."

"Okay, as you wish. Follow me."

As Mr. X stood up, Roy subtly moved closer, his smart gun concealed in his hand, pointed directly at Mr. X's back. Mr. X, sensing danger, instinctively reached inside his jacket for his own weapon.

"No, no, don't even try," Roy hissed, his voice dangerously low. "Now, do exactly as I say, or you'll be dead."

Roy and Sofia swiftly moved, guiding Mr. X and Hasan towards the back exit, avoiding Mr. X's bodyguards stationed at the front. As they emerged, Richard pulled up in the tinted van, the side door sliding open silently. Hasan and a surprised Mr. X were quickly ushered inside.

Back at the safe house, the interrogation began. Roy faced Mr. X.

"So, Mr. X, tell me your real name."

Mr. X smirked. "Roy, you didn't recognize me?"

"How do you know my name?" Roy demanded, a knot of unease tightening in his stomach.

Mr. X removed his hat and sunglasses. Roy's breath hitched.

"Wait a minute… you were my Dad's partner, Brian McQueen! But you were killed in a boat accident, declared dead! Your body was never found…"

"I had to stage my death," Brian sneered, his eyes cold. "So I could sell the weapon your father built without any… complications."

Understanding crashed over Roy like a tidal wave. "So, you're the one who stole my father's device! And… and you were there that night! When Dad got the alert, he caught you stealing the EMP device… and you're the one who killed him!"

A surge of raw anger propelled Roy forward. He lunged at Brian, but John and Richard swiftly intervened, holding him back.

"I'll kill you, you son of a bitch! You're finished!" Roy roared, struggling against their grip.

Richard managed to pull Roy out of the interrogation room, his voice calm but firm. "Roy, calm down. We need to find that weapon. By the way, what exactly *was* the weapon your father built?"

Roy took a deep breath, trying to regain control. "Before he was killed, my father completed a highly dangerous weapon for the US Department of Defense. It's a small but incredibly powerful EMP device. If it detonates, all electronic devices within a 250-mile radius will be fried, completely useless. Brian was my father's partner. When he found out about the EMP, he killed Dad and took it. Staging his own death was just a way to disappear."

"Man, that's incredibly dangerous! It could cause widespread chaos, cripple our entire infrastructure," Richard exclaimed, his face grim. "Roy, we *have* to find that device."

"I have a plan," Roy said, his eyes hardening with determination. "But you have to trust me and back me up."

"What is it?"

Roy leaned in and whispered his plan to Richard. They both re-entered the interrogation room where Brian sat, a smug look on his face.

"Now tell me, Brian, where the hell did you hide that EMP device?" Richard demanded.

"Sorry, Roy, Richard," Brian sneered. "After everything I went through to get my hands on this, you think I'll just tell you? Forget it."

"Brian, I'm asking you one last time," Roy said, his voice dangerously quiet. "Just tell us, otherwise..."

"Otherwise what, Roy? You're not exactly in a position to negotiate."

Rage flared in Roy's eyes. He swiftly drew his smart gun from a hidden holster near his ankle, pointing it directly at Brian. "Tell me where that device is, or I swear I'll kill you."

"You won't kill me, Roy," Brian scoffed. "I know you. You don't have the guts."

"Don't test me," Roy growled, his finger tightening on the trigger. "Tell me now, or I'm counting to three. One... two..."

Richard stepped forward forcefully, trying to intervene. "What are you doing, Roy? Put down your gun, or I'll have to draw mine."

"No, Richard! I have to kill this bastard! He murdered my father! I'm going to have my revenge, no matter what!"

"Stop it, Roy! Don't act like a child! Lower your weapon now!"

"Never!" Roy swung the gun towards Richard. "If you try to stop me, I'll have to shoot you, Richard. Sorry."

"What are you doing? Lower your gun! Have you lost your mind?" Richard exclaimed, his hand hovering over his own weapon.

Sofia, Max, and John watched the escalating confrontation, their faces etched with shock and tension. Suddenly, Roy pulled the trigger. A deafening shot rang out, and Richard crumpled to the floor.

"Roy! What have you done?! You killed Richard!" Sofia screamed, her voice filled with horror.

Seeing Richard lying motionless on the ground, a pool of red spreading beneath him, fear finally gripped Brian. *If he could do that to his own teammate, what will he do to me?*

Roy turned his gun towards Brian, his eyes blazing. Brian, terrified, blurted out, "No, no, please don't! I'll tell you where the device is!"

"Tell me fast!" Roy snarled.

"I've hidden it in the house where I'm staying. There's a small room behind the closet. You can open it with a switch behind the hanging clothes."

"Give me the location! What's the address?"

"It's at 201, B&B Apartment on Rue Desaix road, near the Eiffel Tower."

"Okay, Richard, end of the act. We've got the location."

Richard opened his eyes, a wry smile on his face. He stood up and began wiping the red liquid – clearly fake blood – from his shirt. Sofia, Max, John, Mike, and even a bewildered Brian stared in disbelief.

"You piece of shit! You tricked me!" Brian exclaimed, his face contorted with fury.

"Yes, you bastard," Roy spat. "Just like you tricked my father. But don't worry, I will still have my revenge."

Leaving a furious Brian behind, Roy and his team raced out of the interrogation room, heading for the address Brian had provided.

As they reached the apartment building, Roy and Sofia went inside while Max and John waited in the car.

"Max, John, stay here and watch the entrance for any trouble. I'll call if we need you."

"Yeah, we've got it covered," Max confirmed.

Roy and Sofia ascended to the second floor and found apartment number 201. The door was locked. Roy kicked it open with a sharp blow, drew his smart gun, and cautiously entered the flat, Sofia right behind him.

They systematically searched the apartment.

"Kitchen is clear."

"Room is clear."

"Storeroom is clear too," Roy reported.

They entered the bedroom and found the closet. It was locked. Roy yanked it open with a forceful jerk, revealing a small switch hidden behind the clothes. He flipped it, and a hidden door in the wall swung open, revealing a small room. Inside, two identical EMP devices sat on a table. Roy frowned.

"Sofia, my father only built one E-BOMB. How did he make another one?"

"I don't know. Maybe he hired someone to reverse engineer it and build a second one."

"Hmm, let me check if they're working," Roy said, reaching for one of the devices.

"Are you sure that's a good idea? Let's just grab them and get out of here," Sofia urged.

"No, we need to be sure. What if Brian was trying to mislead us, planting these fakes as a decoy? Better to check."

"At least ask Richard first," Sofia suggested.

"You call him and ask. Meanwhile, let me try to power one up."

Sofia contacted Richard. "Richard, Roy wants to check if the EMP weapon starts. He wants to confirm if it's real or a fake."

"Okay, but handle it with extreme care! Do *not* activate the launch sequence!" Richard stressed.

"Yeah, don't worry, we'll be careful."

Roy examined the E-BOMB, finding a separate controller beside it. "Sofia, there's a green button on this controller. Let's try pressing it."

"Okay, let's do it."

As Roy pressed the button, a screen on the EMP device flickered to life, displaying the message "Configuring the weapon." But after a few seconds, an error message appeared: "Unable to configure, program circuit missing."

"What's this error? It says a circuit is missing."

"Brian might have the missing circuit and didn't tell us," Sofia speculated.

"Wait a minute," Roy said, his eyes scanning the controller. "There's an empty slot beneath it. I think I've seen a shape like this somewhere before…"

"Think fast, Roy! We don't have much time!"

"Yeah… let me think… Yeah! I remember!"

Roy reached under his shirt and pulled out the small circuit attached to his neck chain.

"What are you doing? What is that?" Sofia asked, bewildered.

"This is the missing piece! I bet my father took it out for safety, in case the device fell into the wrong hands. Let's try attaching it."

"Do it quickly!"

Roy carefully inserted the circuit into the slot. As soon as it clicked into place, the screen on the E-BOMB displayed: "Configuration complete. You can activate now."

"Yes! It's working! I didn't even realize I had the key all along," Roy exclaimed.

"Now press that red button and switch it off! Let's get out of here!" Sofia urged.

"Yeah, but I guess Brian was planning to sell it incomplete. Without this, it's useless. Anyway, let's take both E-BOMBS."

As they picked up the devices, Roy's phone rang. It was Richard.

"Roy, our secure facility has been compromised! Five heavily armed men attacked and took Brian!"

"What?! How did this happen? How did they know about our safe house?" Roy demanded, his voice filled with alarm.

"His security guard had unknowingly made him wear a location tracker in his chain. That's how they found him. Get out of there immediately! He might be heading your way. He left fifteen minutes ago, but we couldn't call you because of the breach."

"Okay, okay, we're leaving now!"

As they turned to leave the apartment, Brian stood in the doorway with five heavily armed men flanking him.

"Stop, Roy! Put down those E-BOMBS now! Otherwise, you both will lose your lives!"

"Okay, okay, don't shoot!" Roy said, his hands raised.

"Wait… what is that circuit?" Brian's eyes fell on the exposed component on the controller. "Have you tried to start the device?"

Brian snatched the controller from Roy's hand and pressed the green button. The screen on the EMP device immediately lit up. He laughed triumphantly.

"Very well, Roy! Congratulations! You just found the missing piece! Now I'll clone this, and my two E-BOMBS will be ready to launch! Now, kill these two bastards!"

One of the guards stepped forward, raising his weapon. Suddenly, a shot rang out from behind, and the guard crumpled to the floor, a bullet hole in his head. Chaos erupted. Everyone scrambled for cover, trying to locate the shooter. Roy and Sofia instantly drew their smart guns, locking onto the two remaining guards and firing. The smart bullets unerringly found their targets, eliminating the other two guards. A figure in a mask entered the apartment, gesturing for Roy and Sofia to follow. They didn't hesitate, rushing downstairs with the masked individual and jumping into the car where Max and John were waiting.

"John, drive fast! We're under attack!" Roy yelled.

John slammed on the accelerator, the car screeching away from the apartment building.

As they sped through the Parisian streets, two black SUVs appeared in their rear-view mirror, relentlessly tailing them.

"We're being followed!" John exclaimed.

"Full throttle, John!" Roy commanded.

The car surged forward. Suddenly, a man leaned out of the window of the lead SUV and opened fire. Bullets shattered the rear windshield, and everyone ducked for cover.

"Take this gun and start shooting, Roy!" John shouted, shoving an M4 Carbine into Roy's hands.

Roy braced himself against the broken windshield and unleashed a barrage of fire at the pursuing SUV. His shots shattered the front windshield. After a few more rounds, he aimed carefully and blew out a tire. The SUV swerved wildly, losing control and colliding violently with a truck approaching from the opposite direction.

The second SUV took the lead and continued the chase. A man in the passenger seat produced a rocket launcher, aiming at their car. Just as he fired, John executed a sharp left turn, the missile slamming into an empty building with a deafening explosion. Roy stood up again, firing steadily at the SUV. His bullets cracked the front windshield. He took aim and fired a single shot at the driver. The bullet found its mark, and the SUV swerved erratically, rolling four or five times before crashing into the road divider. John floored the accelerator, leaving the mangled wreckage behind.

Once they were a safe distance away, Roy turned to the masked figure in the back seat.

"Who are you? And why did you help us?"

The figure's voice was strangely familiar. "Hi, Roy. Remember my voice?"

"First Brian, and now this person knows me too? Oh god. Hey, how do you know me? And wait… I *have* heard that voice before. Take off your mask."

"Are you sure?" the figure asked hesitantly.

"Yeah, yeah, just take it off."

The masked figure slowly removed their mask. Roy stared in stunned silence. It was…

Chapter 13: The Ex-Help.

The masked figure lowered their hands, revealing a face Roy hadn't seen in years, yet recognized instantly. It was Christina, his ex-girlfriend. Roy was stunned.

"Christina! What are you doing here?"

"What? You're not happy to see me?" she asked, a hint of playful hurt in her voice.

"No, nothing like that," Roy stammered, still processing the shock. "I just… didn't expect to meet you here, under these circumstances, after so long."

"Wait a minute, you two know each other?" Sofia interjected, her eyes narrowed with suspicion.

"He didn't tell you all about me?" Christina asked, a wry smile playing on her lips.

"No," Sofia replied curtly.

"I *used* to be Roy's girlfriend," Christina explained, her gaze softening as she looked at him. "But we broke up because he chose his career over me."

"You also know *why* I chose this career, Christina," Roy countered, a touch of defensiveness in his tone.

"Oh, you two, please stop," John said, breaking the awkward tension. "This isn't the time for a relationship recap. Christina, tell us, why did you save us?"

"I came to Sam Hopkins' place to steal that E-BOMB so it wouldn't fall into the wrong hands," she explained. "But when I got there, I saw Roy in danger. That's why I intervened."

"Wait, who is Sam Hopkins?" Roy asked, confused.

"The one in the cream suit."

"His name is Brian McQueen, not Sam Hopkins."

"No, I've known him for so long. His name is definitely Sam. And he killed my family."

"He might have changed his name after staging the boat accident," Roy speculated. "But why did Brian kill your family?"

Christina's expression darkened, her eyes hardening with grief. "My father was a weapon specialist. He helped design many weapons for the US military. Sam somehow found out about my father and abducted him, forcing him to work on that EMP device Roy's father built. He couldn't activate it, so Brian forced him to reverse engineer it and make a copy. After a lot of effort, my father succeeded in building the same device, but he couldn't activate it without that circuit. To cover his tracks, he killed my father and everyone who knew about the weapon. He killed my whole family. Somehow, I survived. I trained hard and started hunting for my father's killer. About a month ago, I got a tip that he was hiding in Paris, so I've been tailing him ever since."

"But why didn't you kill him yourself?" Sofia asked, her suspicion still evident.

"He's always surrounded by bodyguards," Christina replied. "And I also wanted to find the E-BOMB so it couldn't be used for anything terrible. When I heard he'd been abducted, I thought it was the perfect opportunity to search his house for the missing weapon. But when I was about to enter, I saw Roy at gunpoint, so I reacted immediately and saved you two. But tell me, Roy, why were you at Brian's mercy?"

"We're all CIA agents," Roy explained. "We found out that Brian McQueen was trying to sell the device to Bashir Hashemi, and they're planning a massive attack on US soil. We only knew about one E-BOMB before, but I don't know why Bashir is interested in two."

"We need to confront Brian about that," Christina said, her voice firm. "But the problem is, he's already escaped. We need to find out where he went."

"Why don't you work with us?" Roy suggested. "We could use an extra hand."

Sofia's surprise was evident. "What! Her?? Roy, you can't be serious! She's not CIA! We're not allowed to do that!"

"Yeah, I know the rules," Roy conceded. "But this could be in our favor. Christina knows more about Brian than we do. She could be a valuable asset. I'll make Richard say yes."

"Roy's right," Max agreed. "We're running out of time, and we can't afford to lose more ground. Christina could be a real help."

"Okay then," John said, starting the engine. "Drive fast, let's get to the station immediately."

They arrived at the CIA station to find Richard, Mike, and Anton already there, their faces etched with concern.

"Thank god, you're all right! Tell me, where's the E-BOMB?" Richard asked urgently.

"After you told us Brian escaped, he went straight to his house," Roy explained. "He got there just as we were about to leave. His men took us at gunpoint. Brian also figured out that the EMP weapon could be activated now that it's fully configured. Just as they were about to pull the trigger, Christina saved us, and we got out of there immediately. And… sorry, we also lost the EMP weapon. One more thing, Richard, there are *two* EMP weapons, not one."

"What! Two EMP weapons? That's incredibly dangerous! And by the way, who is Christina? And what's she doing here?" Anton asked, his eyes shifting between Christina and Roy.

"Brian killed her entire family," Roy explained. "She came to Brian's house to find the weapon. She saw us at gunpoint and immediately shot the guard, saving our lives."

"She's Roy's ex-girlfriend," Sofia added, a hint of something unreadable in her voice.

Roy shot Sofia a warning glance.

"What! We need to be careful," Sofia muttered.

"Wait! Ex-girlfriend? Strange she saved you, not killed you," Richard joked, trying to lighten the tense atmosphere.

"We separated without any drama," Christina replied, her gaze meeting Roy's. "And I still care about him."

"Richard, I'm thinking of letting Christina join us for this mission," Roy said, his voice serious. "She knows more about Brian than we do, and they're already two steps ahead. She could be a valuable asset to our team."

Richard considered this, his brow furrowed. "Hmm, good idea, potentially. But I don't want any personal vendettas affecting the mission."

"We're both fine," Roy assured him. "No need to worry, right, Christina?"

"Yeah," she confirmed.

"Now we're back to square one," Anton sighed. "We need to find those weapons before they can be used."

"Don't worry," Christina said, a determined glint in her eyes. "Before he took the weapon, I attached GPS trackers to *both* of them. Max, can you please track them?"

"Let me try," Max replied, his fingers flying across his keyboard.

After a moment, his face fell. "I'm unable to track the devices."

"They might have kept the E-BOMBS in some kind of anti-tracking box," Christina speculated.

"Could be," Max agreed. "But I'll keep an eye on the tracker's signal. If they somehow open the box, we'll get their exact location."

"Okay, on it."

"Mike, contact airport security and inform Interpol about Brian," Richard instructed. "If he's already flown out of the country or tries to, we need to know."

"Okay, I'll inform everyone," Mike replied, picking up his phone.

Meanwhile, Roy went to the station kitchen to grab some coffee, and Christina followed him.

"Roy, how are you really?" she asked, her voice softer now.

"I'm… good, Christina. How are you?"

"I'm doing okay. By the way, you joined the Navy SEALs! How did you end up in the CIA?"

"I was in the SEALs for a few years, but based on my performance, I was transferred to the CIA for this mission. So now, I'm a CIA agent. What about you, Christina? I tried calling you years ago, when I was in training, but your number was disconnected."

"Yeah, I changed my number," she explained. "Some creep got hold of it and was harassing me, so I switched it. Nothing important."

"Okay… so, are you in a relationship?"

"No, Roy. Haven't found anyone quite like you," she said, her gaze lingering on him. "What about you?"

"Same, Christina. Haven't really had the time to think about relationships."

"Yeah, right," she chuckled softly. "Well, I'm happy to see you after so long, Roy."

"Me too, Christina."

Christina leaned in and placed a soft kiss on Roy's lips. "Is there anywhere private we can go for a moment?" she whispered.

Roy led her to a dusty storage room. The state of the room seemed to fade into insignificance as Christina immediately grabbed him, kissing him passionately. Roy returned her embrace, pulling her close. Clothes were shed, and soon they were lost in a fervent embrace, years of separation melting away in their shared intimacy. They held each other tightly, oblivious to the urgent mission that awaited them.

"That felt good, Roy," Christina murmured after a long moment. "After so long."

"Yeah," Roy breathed, "like heaven."

After a while, they emerged from the storage room and returned to the surveillance room.

"Where were you both?" Sofia asked, a hint of suspicion in her tone.

"Nothing," Roy said casually. "We were just in the kitchen, having coffee and catching up. We haven't seen each other in years."

"Okay… coffee," Sofia repeated, unconvinced.

"Yes! Coffee, Sofia!"

An hour later, Mike received an update.

"Richard, we got information from the airport about Brian. He already flew out in a private jet, and we don't know his destination."

"When did he leave?"

"About an hour ago."

Three tense hours passed. Suddenly, a faint beep emanated from Max's computer screen. The tracker on one of the E-BOMBS had sprung to life.

"Roy! Richard! We've got a signal!" Max exclaimed.

Roy and Richard rushed to Max's station, their eyes glued to the screen.

"Where is the location?" Richard asked urgently.

"It shows Zurich," Max replied.

"Get ready, everyone! We're going to Zurich!" Richard declared. "Anton, contact Langley and tell them to activate agents in Zurich. Ask them to trace Bashir Hashemi and Rashid Mazdani. If we find them, we find Brian."

"You all leave immediately. Your arrangements will be ready as soon as you reach Zurich," Anton assured them.

"Thanks, Anton. It's been a… pleasure working with you. See you soon."

"Goodbye, and good luck."

Roy, Christina, Sofia, Max, John, Richard, and Mike immediately headed to the airport. Their private jet was waiting. They quickly boarded and set course for Zurich, Switzerland. Max continuously monitored the faint tracker signal. Meanwhile, CIA assets in Zurich were activated, pulling every available piece of information on Bashir Hashemi. A nervous tension filled the jet, especially for Roy, who felt a pang of guilt for inadvertently arming the EMP devices.

"I shouldn't have inserted that missing circuit and started that weapon," Roy muttered, his brow furrowed. "Because of me, they now have two active E-BOMBS. It was a stupid mistake."

"Don't beat yourself up, Roy," Richard said, placing a hand on his shoulder. "You were just trying to confirm. I probably would have done the same. Just focus on how to get them back."

"He's right, Roy," Christina added softly.

"Hmm, you're right, Richard," Roy conceded. "Better to focus on the mission than dwell on the past we can't change."

Four hours later, they landed at Zurich Airport. Two cars waited on the tarmac to take them to the CIA base in Zurich. As soon as the jet stopped, they disembarked and piled into the vehicles. A mere twenty minutes later, they arrived at the base, where they were greeted by Rob Thomson, the CIA Station Chief of Zurich.

"Welcome to Zurich. I received a call from Langley. I've already activated our assets. They're retrieving information ASAP. We should have the exact whereabouts of Bashir Hashemi within the hour."

"Good. I want five extra agents with us for backup," Richard requested.

"Don't worry. I'll arrange my best men for you. Take some rest if you need it."

An hour later, one of the assets arrived with the crucial information and briefed Rob. Rob immediately summoned the team to a mission control room.

"Guys, we've located Rashid Mazdani, Bashir Hashemi's right-hand man. According to our source, he's meeting a man named Sam Hopkins – real name Brian McQueen – at an empty warehouse outside Zurich. Brian will deliver the weapon to Rashid there. The meeting is happening at 3:00 PM, which is exactly two hours from now."

"Rob, tell those five agents to get equipped and ready," Richard ordered. "Meanwhile, show me the weapon room. This is going to be messy. Everyone, gear up!"

Rob led them to a hidden weapon room beneath the ground. It was a high-tech arsenal, with various firearms mounted on the walls and racks, along with grenade launchers, bazookas, grenades, and a vast supply of ammunition, including rounds capable of piercing bulletproof shields.

Roy, Christina, Sofia, Max, and John armed themselves with guns, knives, and their existing gadgets. Richard and Mike decided to stay in the control room to monitor the mission.

With half an hour remaining, the team and the five additional agents were en route to the empty warehouse on the outskirts of Zurich. As they arrived, Max deployed a drone to scout the location, analyzing entry and exit points and potential threats.

The warehouse stood in an open field of lush green grass. It was a large, dilapidated wooden barn with broken windows and a thick layer of dust. Examining the drone footage, Max reported, "Entries and exits seem straightforward. And here's the internal layout."

"We'll operate in two-person teams, along with the five extra agents," Roy outlined the plan. "Christina and I will attack from the front. I want two pairs of snipers on the first floor. John, with one of the agents, you'll use the grenade launcher to create a diversion. Sofia and Max will cover the exit. The other two agents will be our backup. But listen carefully: don't attack until I give the signal. The main objective is to retrieve those two E-BOMBS. Whoever gets to them first, grab them and get out immediately, heading back to the CIA station. The rest of us will handle the situation."

They infiltrated the warehouse, taking up concealed positions. Their car was parked a distance away to avoid detection.

"Everyone ready?" Roy whispered over the radio.

"Me and Max in position," Sofia replied.

"We are in position," confirmed one of the sniper teams.

"Me and my partner are ready," John reported.

"Backup ready, call us when needed," the remaining agents confirmed.

"It's 3:00 PM," Roy announced. "Max, any visuals from the drone?"

"No, not yet. Wait… three black Range Rovers are approaching the warehouse."

"Guys! Get ready!"

Three black Range Rovers entered the warehouse grounds. Ten armed bodyguards emerged and took defensive positions around the vehicles. Rashid remained inside one of the cars.

"Guys, three more black G-Wagons are on their way. Looks like Brian McQueen."

"Alert! Our target is arriving. Remember, our priority is the E-BOMBS. Whoever gets them first, vanish as fast as you can. The rest of us will handle the situation," Roy reiterated.

Three black G-Wagons pulled up to the warehouse. Ten more bodyguards, presumably Brian's, exited the vehicles. Finally, Brian emerged with his accountant. At the same moment, Rashid also stepped out of his Range Rover with his own accountant.

"Hello, Mr. Rashid. Your toys are ready," Brian said, a smug grin on his face.

"Very good. I heard the CIA arrested you," Rashid replied, his voice carrying a hint of amusement.

"Yeah, they took me, but they won't be holding onto me for long. As you can see, I have a loyal army of bodyguards with me."

"Great. Now, let's do business," Rashid said, his Arabic accent thick.

"Sure. Guards! Bring out the devices."

Brian's guards produced two cases, opened them, and displayed the EMP devices.

"Very well. Now, show me how they work," Rashid instructed.

"You just have to press this green button to start it," Brian explained, pointing to the controller. "And on this screen, you can set the timer and detonate it whenever you want."

While examining one of the devices, Rashid noticed a small red light blinking continuously beneath the machine.

"Wait, what is this blinking?" he asked, pointing at the light.

Brian saw it and quickly plucked it off. It was a tracking device. *If I tell him it's a CIA tracker, he might cancel the deal,* Brian thought quickly. Instead, he said, "It's a tracking device. If anyone tries to steal my device, I can track it."

"Remove this device. I don't want anyone tracking it," Rashid ordered.

Brian crushed the tracker under his heel.

"Now, first, my payment," he said, extending his hand.

"Yeah, sure."

Rashid instructed his accountant to transfer one billion dollars to Brian's offshore account. Brian, in turn, ordered his man to open his laptop to verify the transfer.

Seeing them engrossed in the transaction, Roy decided it was time to initiate the mission.

"Guys, be ready," he whispered into his comms. "On my count, snipers will take out the guards. One will target Rashid's guard, the other Brian's. Christina and I will engage Brian's remaining guards. Max and Sofia, you take on Rashid's. John, listen carefully: as soon as the snipers fire, you launch a grenade at one of their cars. Get ready, everyone. On my count… three… two… one… and shoot!"

Chapter 14: Betrayal.

Roy and his team were about to attack when Rashid and Brian's guards suddenly spotted them. They were caught completely off guard. Their hands were zip-tied, and they were dragged before Brian and Rashid.

"Well, well, well, Roy," Brian sneered. "It would have been better for you and your team if you hadn't come looking for us. Now you're all in deep trouble. By the way, have you met my daughter?"

"You have a daughter?" Roy asked, his voice filled with disbelief.

"Yes, my dear boy. And you've already met her." Brian gestured towards Christina.

Roy's eyes widened, a sense of dread washing over him. "Is it true, Christina?"

"I'm sorry, Roy, but yes, it's true," she confessed, her voice laced with a hint of remorse.

"What! You've been using me this whole time? It was all a lie from the moment we met?" Roy exclaimed, his voice filled with anger and betrayal.

"I am sorry, Roy, but not all of it was fake," Christina said softly. "I really did fall in love with you. That's why my father pulled me away."

"I made Christina fall in love with you so that you would tell her about that missing circuit from the device," Brian explained, his voice cold and calculating. "But I guess you didn't know about it then. So, to maintain my cover, I ordered Christina to break up with you and come back to me. After you caught me in Paris, and after my guards released me from your base, I immediately contacted Christina and staged your rescue. I was confident that seeing Christina after so long would soften you, and you would definitely invite her to join the mission. And you did. Christina was a great help, giving me all the inside information. I'm proud of my daughter. And yeah, thanks a lot, Roy, for retrieving that missing circuit and activating the EMP weapon. I didn't expect it, but you made my work easy."

"You bitch! You fooled me! You used me!" Roy roared, his voice shaking with rage. "If my hands weren't tied, I would kill you both!"

Roy was devastated, the betrayal from the woman he loved cutting deep. He struggled to control his fury, wanting nothing more than to make Brian and Christina pay.

"Why did you kill my father?" Roy demanded, his voice trembling. "If you wanted the device, you should have just taken it, but why did you kill him?"

"He caught me stealing the device and tried to stop me," Brian said, his voice devoid of emotion. "We fought, and it got ugly. I had to kill him in self-defense. But all I can say is that your father was a genius. He did a great job hiding that circuit. I searched everywhere for it after his murder. I even sent professional thieves to your place, but they couldn't find it. But thanks to you, Roy, you made my work easy."

"Brian, your mission is never going to succeed," Richard spat, his eyes filled with hatred.

"My mission is already over. I've sold my device, and I have the money. Now, enough of this nonsense. Guards, kill them all after we leave."

"No! Dad, you said you wouldn't kill Roy!" Christina protested, her voice filled with desperation.

"Sorry, dear, but I can't leave any loose ends."

"But at least tell me what you're going to do with those two E-BOMBS," Roy pleaded, hoping to buy some time.

"Let's tell him, Brian. It's okay, he's going to die anyway. Let's grant his last wish."

"Okay," Brian agreed.

"In three days, at 5:00 PM, we're going to detonate these two E-BOMBS," Brian revealed, a chilling smile spreading across his face. "One in the air from a plane at around 35,000 feet. At that time, around 50 planes will be flying within the blast radius. It will disable all the electronics in those planes, and they will literally fall from the sky to the ground in a densely populated city area. More than 50,000 people will die with just one EMP blast. And at the same time, we'll detonate the other E-BOMB at the Pentagon, crippling your entire military command. It will be the biggest attack in US history. You all are going to suffer very badly."

"Brian, have you gone mad? Don't you have a heart? Don't you see what they're going to do to your country?" Richard exclaimed, his voice filled with horror.

"I don't care. I've got a lucrative offer of a lifetime."

"Sir, the transfer is complete," Brian's accountant announced.

"See? I have a billion dollars with me. I'll enjoy the rest of my life somewhere with a new name and identity. Okay then, we're leaving now. Let's go, Christina."

"Dad, let me say goodbye to Roy," Christina said, her eyes filled with a mixture of sadness and guilt.

Christina hugged Roy without his consent, and as she did, she subtly slipped a small knife into his zip-tied hands. Roy was surprised by her unexpected help. She then left with her father. Rashid also departed with the two deadly devices. Richard had been watching the entire scene unfold through their body cams. When they were taken hostage, he immediately dispatched a team of twenty agents to rescue them.

After Brian and Rashid left the warehouse, the guards lined them up to be executed. Somehow, Roy managed to cut through his zip-ties with the knife Christina had given him. He quickly took out the blast ring Mark had given him, twisted it, and threw it at the guards who were about to pull the trigger. The blast from the ring killed three guards instantly.

"Hurry up! Everyone, grab a gun and take cover!" Roy shouted.

Everyone scrambled for cover, and a fierce firefight erupted. Roy, Sofia, Max, and John used their smart guns, firing from behind cover, easily taking out the remaining guards.

"Wow, I love this gun," Max exclaimed, impressed by its efficiency.

Soon, the team of twenty trained agents arrived, reinforcing Roy's team and quickly neutralizing all of Rashid and Brian's men.

"Thanks, guys, for saving us. Now, please take us to Richard immediately," Roy said, his voice urgent.

They all returned to the CIA station, where Richard was waiting. Roy, Max, John, and Sofia were all injured and dishevelled.

"Thank God you're all alive," Richard said, relief evident in his voice. "I sent the rescue team as soon as I saw you getting captured on your body cams."

"Thanks, Richard, for having our backs," Roy replied.

"Roy, your emotions really screwed us over," Richard said sternly.

"I'm sorry, Richard. I know I endangered all of you because of my feelings, and I'm ready to face any disciplinary actions taken against me."

"We'll deal with that later. We don't have time for this now. I've heard about their evil plan. I've already alerted Homeland Security and the FBI about the threat. They're all on high alert. You guys clean up, and let's get back to DC immediately. We have to find those bastards before they launch their attack."

Roy, Sofia, Max, and John cleaned themselves up and immediately headed to the airport for their private jet. They boarded and set course for Washington DC. On the plane, Roy asked Richard, "Richard, what can we do now? We're back to square one."

"Homeland Security, the FBI, and the CIA are all working together to identify anyone linked to this," Richard explained. "The CIA is closely monitoring for any chatter about the attack. I'm sure we'll find a lead."

"Rashid is personally handling this operation. I guess if we track the security camera footage from Zurich, we might be able to figure out where they went," Max suggested.

"Let me access their traffic cam footage," Richard said, his fingers flying across his laptop.

"Do it fast," Roy urged.

"Got it," Richard announced. "I found Rashid's Range Rover. He drove away from the warehouse and headed towards a private airstrip."

"If we contact that private airstrip, we can get information about his plane and where he's traveling," Roy suggested.

Meanwhile, when Rashid reached the airport, he transferred the two E-BOMBS to a cargo plane carrying medical equipment to the United States. This allowed the weapons to enter the country without raising suspicion.

Max hacked into the private airstrip's system and found the flight that took off around the time Rashid arrived at the airport.

"Roy, I got access to the airport system. There's only one flight that took off around the time Rashid was there."

"Yeah, I bet that's the one."

"What's the tail number of that plane?" Richard asked.

"KR163012."

"Find out who owns the plane."

"It belongs to a shell corporation. There's no way to track the owner."

"Immediately send a message to all airports in the United States," Richard ordered. "If this plane lands, detain everyone on board immediately. Also, send images of Bashir Hashemi and Rashid Mazdani to all agencies and alert them."

Bashir Hashemi had already entered the United States using a disguise, a fake passport, and a new identity. He gathered his team and took refuge in an abandoned factory outside Washington. He disguised his men as hospital officials and sent them to the airport to retrieve the cargo containing the E-BOMBS.

Roy and his team landed in Washington, where two cars were waiting to pick them up. They were transported to the CIA facility in Washington. News of the impending threat had reached the President, who ordered immediate action. He called an emergency meeting at the White House, inviting Richard and Roy, as they were leading the mission. They went directly to the White House.

At the White House, all the top officials were in the conference room waiting for the President. The President entered the room, and Richard and Roy joined him.

"Sorry we're late. We just landed from Zurich and came straight here," Richard apologized.

"Have a seat immediately," the CIA Director said, his tone urgent.

They sat down, and Richard whispered to Roy, "Don't say anything until you're told to. Understood?"

"Understood," Roy replied.

"Tell me the exact nature of the threat," the President demanded.

"Richard will explain it to you. He's in charge of the mission," the CIA Director said.

Richard stood up to brief the President. "As we all know, the Iranian terrorist organization SCRIOS is planning an attack on the United States. My team went to Paris and Zurich to neutralize the threat, but the enemy managed to escape. As far as we know, they plan to detonate two EMP weapons, also known as E-BOMBS, in Washington. One will be detonated in the air from a plane at around 35,000 feet. At that time, approximately 50 aircraft will be within the blast radius. The blast will disable all electronic devices within a 250-mile radius, causing all those aircraft to crash into densely populated areas. Our estimated casualties are above 50,000 people. It would be an avion menace. The other E-BOMB will be detonated at the Pentagon, crippling our entire military command. All of Washington, including other major cities within a 250-mile radius, will be blacked out, with no phone service or emergency services. If this attack happens, it will be the greatest catastrophe in human history. There will be chaos throughout the country."

"Where did they get these E-BOMBS?" the President asked, his voice grave.

"The weapon was sold by our own citizen, Brian McQueen. He stole it from his partner, Dr. Victor Spectre, and killed him. Dr. Victor built this weapon for our Department of Defence. Brian stole it and staged his own death, vanishing from the states and assuming a new identity. He found a lucrative offer from SCRIOS and sold them these two weapons for a billion dollars. Meet the man leading the ground team of this mission, Roy Spectre, son of Dr. Victor Spectre," Richard explained.

"Sorry for your loss, Roy. Do your best to neutralize this threat," the President said, his eyes filled with concern.

"I will try my best, sir," Roy replied, his voice filled with determination.

"I want every agency in the state working to neutralize these threats. Increase security at the Pentagon and secure and check all airports. You all have carte blanche," the President ordered.

"Yes, Mr. President. We're doing our best," the CIA Director assured him.

"This meeting is over. I want hourly reports on this mission."

After the meeting, Roy and Richard returned to the CIA facility in Washington. It was a bustling place, filled with employees and expert analysts. Sofia, Max, and John were already there. Max was trying to track down any leads connected to Bashir Hashemi.

An hour later, Max received an alert: private aircraft "KR163012" had landed at the Washington Airport private strip. Security authorities immediately detained the plane and its belongings. However, when the airport police searched the jet for Rashid, they found only the pilot. The pilot claimed he was ordered to bring the aircraft to Washington Airport and knew nothing more.

"Roy, airport security didn't find Rashid on that plane," Max reported, his face grim.

"What! We saw him go to the airport. I guess he suspected we were tracking him. He vanished and sent an empty plane as a decoy," Roy deduced.

They all began analyzing their existing leads. Tension filled the air, with only 48 hours remaining before the planned attack. All agencies were working tirelessly to find any clues, canvassing suspicious areas in and around Washington. All passengers arriving in the United States were being thoroughly checked. It seemed these 48 hours would be the longest of their lives.

Chapter 15: The Wanted List.

Bashir Hashemi received a call from his men detailing the arrival of the medical cargo concealing the two E-BOMBS. He dispatched a team disguised as hospital personnel, complete with forged identification.

"Retrieve that cargo from the airport," Bashir instructed. "Rashid is also arriving. Bring him back with you. Ensure your disguises are convincing."

His men proceeded to the airport. Their infiltration, courtesy of Bashir's planted operative within the airport staff, allowed them to secure the cargo with ease. They collected the two E-BOMBS and then picked up Rashid. He carried a fake passport and identification bearing a different name. Bashir's men transported Rashid and the cargo to a secluded warehouse, where he met Bashir.

"Marhaba! Rashid, how was your flight?" Bashir greeted him.

"It was smooth," Rashid replied, "undertaken with considerable precaution. Our strategy of sending an empty plane proved successful. I anticipated they would be tracking my vehicle, so after reaching the private airstrip, I didn't board. I adopted a disguise, returned to Zurich Airport, and with the forged documents, entered Washington."

"Excellent work."

"So, how will we execute the mission?" Rashid inquired.

"You will lead the assault on the Pentagon," Bashir stated, "and I will personally command the mid-air operation. Four of us will conduct the aerial strike. After detonating the E-BOMB, the pilot will engage the autopilot, and we will all parachute out mid-air. Rashid, you will undertake your mission with one of our men. I have already placed an operative inside the Pentagon; he will disable the air conditioning system. We have rerouted their air conditioning contractor's number to our phone. When they call to complain, you will go in disguise as a repairman. We have painted a van to match their contractor's vehicle and acquired stolen IDs from two of their technicians to create forgeries. Your task is to go with Abu. Once inside, our contact will assist you and guide you to the Pentagon's terrace, where you will detonate the E-BOMB. Immediately after detonation, you both must evacuate as quickly as possible. We will regroup here. As soon as that E-BOMB explodes, we will immediately vanish from D.C. and head towards Chicago, from where we will fly back to Zurich and then return to Iran."

"A brilliant plan," Rashid affirmed. "Inshallah, it will undoubtedly succeed."

As Rashid and Bashir discussed the finer points, a sound from behind the door interrupted them.

"Abu, see who's there," Rashid directed.

Abu moved to the door and caught a glimpse of a figure disappearing.

"Rashid," Abu reported, "I saw a man just now. I believe he overheard our entire conversation."

"Take two men and eliminate him before he can divulge anything," Bashir commanded.

Rashid and Abu got into a car while two other men gave chase on foot, flanking the fleeing individual. As the man attempted to escape through the backyard, they apprehended him. Rashid immediately drew his weapon and fired three shots, ending the man's life. Spotting a parked car, Abu smashed a window, opened the door, dragged the body, and placed it inside. He then doused the vehicle with gasoline, set it ablaze, and they vanished from the scene.

A 911 call reported the burning car with a body inside. A Washington P.D. patrol car and the fire brigade swiftly arrived. After extinguishing the flames, detectives from Washington P.D. began their investigation, led by none other than Captain George Gregor. Seven years prior, George had transferred to D.C. to care for his aging parents, who were facing health issues. His exemplary record quickly propelled him to the rank of Captain. The unusual nature of this case prompted George to personally oversee the investigation.

Arriving at the scene, he observed the charred remains within the vehicle. The body was also partially burned. Medical Examiner Susan arrived and conducted an initial examination, sharing her preliminary findings with Captain George.

"The victim is male, in his thirties, approximately five foot eight inches tall," she stated. "He sustained three gunshot wounds to the chest, likely from a .45 caliber weapon. His fingerprints are destroyed by the fire, so we have no immediate identification. A thorough examination at the lab will provide more definitive answers."

"Understood," George replied. "I'll instruct my detectives to canvass the area and see if anyone witnessed anything suspicious."

One of George's detectives canvassing the neighbourhood found a woman who had seen four men fleeing the backyard of a nearby building, heading north.

"Have that woman work with our sketch artist to create images of the four individuals she saw," George instructed.

George's team provided him with the sketches of the four suspects. He took them back to the police department. As he walked past the "WANTED Criminals" board, his gaze fell upon the photographs of Bashir Hashemi and Rashid Mazdani. One of the sketches bore a striking resemblance to Rashid. George immediately compared the sketch to the photograph. It was a match. He promptly informed the FBI about the suspects and the murder.

The FBI relayed the information about the matching sketch and the murder to the CIA. Richard, in turn, immediately contacted Roy.

"Rashid is here in Washington," Richard reported. "Washington P.D. has a sketch that matches him. He and three accomplices murdered a man, burned the car, and fled the scene."

"Excellent," Roy responded. "We need to move quickly. Only thirty-six hours remain until the anticipated attack. We must apprehend them ASAP."

"I can track them from here using our advanced facial recognition software," Max offered.

"That would be invaluable."

"Alright, I'll call you as soon as I have any updates," Max said.

"In the meantime, let me contact the detective handling the murder case. I'll go there and supervise personally," Roy decided.

Roy proceeded to Washington P.D. and met Captain George Gregor, accompanied by an FBI agent.

"Hello George, I am Roy Spectre, CIA," Roy introduced himself.

"Hello, how can I assist you, Agent Roy?" George inquired.

"Who was murdered, and what happened?"

"We received a 911 call from Branch Avenue regarding a burning car with a deceased individual inside," George explained. "The victim was shot three times in the chest with a .45 caliber weapon. A witness reported seeing four men running north from the crime scene."

"Have you uncovered any leads?"

"Not yet. Our immediate priority is identifying the victim. Once we have that, we can proceed further."

"May I ask you a question?" Roy inquired.

"Certainly."

"Are you in any way related to Victor and Veronica Spectre?"

"Yes, how do you know me?" George asked, surprised.

"I was the one who investigated your father's murder."

"Oh, right. You were in New York, weren't you? How did you end up here in D.C.?"

"My parents were aging and experiencing health issues, so I transferred here to care for them. By the way, I am very sorry for your loss. We explored every possible avenue in your father's case but were unable to find his killer. It remains the only unsolved case in my career."

"Don't worry, Detective," George said. "I've already found my father's killer. He was murdered by my father's partner, Brian McQueen. And you know what? He's already escaped from our custody."

"Oh! I am truly sorry to hear that."

"All I can say is that he is somehow connected to this current incident as well."

As George and Roy were speaking, the autopsy report arrived.

"Roy, the autopsy report is here," George announced. "Dental records have confirmed the victim's identity. His name is Vincent Bodega, and he lived near Branch Avenue."

"Let's go to his residence and speak with Vincent's family about the murder," Roy suggested.

"Alright, let's go."

They drove to Vincent Bodega's house on Branch Avenue, located near the crime scene. Roy considered the possibility of a conspiracy against the victim. He speculated that Rashid's act might have been a necessary consequence – perhaps Vincent had seen or heard something he shouldn't have.

They reached the house and knocked. A brunette woman, around twenty-eight years old and five foot five inches tall, opened the door. Her name was Ariana Bodega.

"Yes, how can I help you?" she asked.

"I am Captain George from Washington P.D., and this is Roy. We are here to ask you some questions about your husband's murder," George stated.

"Yes, please come in."

George and Roy entered a small, single-story home of modest appearance. Toys scattered the floor, and the air carried the faint scent of baby powder and used diapers, suggesting a young child lived there. Roy addressed Ariana.

"Do you have a baby?"

"Yes," she replied, her voice tinged with sadness. "We have a five-month-old daughter. She just lost her father." Tears welled up in her eyes.

"We are deeply sorry for your loss," Roy said gently. "Do you know anyone who might have wanted to harm your husband?"

"No," Ariana insisted. "He was a kind and generous man. He helped everyone in the neighbourhood, as well as our friends and family. Everyone loved Vincent."

"Did he mention where he was going before he was killed?"

"Yes, he said he was going for a short walk and would be back in a few minutes. When he didn't return after almost two hours, I tried calling him, but his phone was off. I then contacted all our close friends and relatives, but no one had seen him. So, I filed a missing person report, and later, your department called to tell me he was dead."

"Did he have any recent arguments or confrontations with anyone?" Roy asked.

"Well, yes," Ariana recalled. "Yesterday, he had an argument with an Arabic man. His van backed into our car, and they had a heated exchange."

"Do you know who this man was?"

"No, I don't."

"What kind of car was he driving?"

"It was a black tinted van, and he seemed very nervous. He immediately gave my husband money for the car repairs and left quickly."

"Would you be able to describe him to our sketch artist?"

"Yes, I can."

They immediately contacted the sketch artist. Ariana provided a detailed description, and within an hour, the sketch was complete. When George saw it, he was stunned. He immediately showed it to Roy.

"Jesus Christ, it's Rashid," George exclaimed. "We've got him."

Roy turned back to Ariana. "Are you absolutely certain you haven't seen this man before that accident? He is a suspect in your husband's murder."

"No, I am positive. I had never seen him before the accident, and I haven't seen him since."

"Okay," Roy acknowledged.

He immediately called Richard to relay the crucial information.

"Richard, we have a lead on Rashid," Roy reported. "Yesterday, the man he murdered had an argument with Rashid after Rashid's van hit his car. We obtained a sketch from the victim's wife, and it's definitely Rashid."

"Excellent! That's a significant breakthrough, Roy. Act fast; we have less than twelve hours to prevent this attack."

"I'm on it."

"Why are the CIA, FBI, and Homeland Security so intensely interested in this homicide, and who exactly is this Rashid?" George inquired.

"I'm sorry, George, that information is confidential," Roy replied.

"I won't be able to provide effective assistance without a clearer understanding of who we're dealing with," George pressed.

"As I said, it's classified, and I won't repeat myself," Roy stated firmly. "Rashid is a dangerous Iranian operative working for SCRIOS, a powerful criminal syndicate with a long-standing vendetta against the United States. They are planning a dangerous attack within the next twelve hours. If we don't apprehend him in time, the entire Washington D.C. area will suffer. We must act swiftly."

"Understood," George said. "Don't worry, we'll find them."

"Are there any CCTV cameras in this vicinity?" Roy asked.

"Let me instruct my detectives to canvass the area again and check for any surveillance cameras around the crime scene and the victim's house," George directed.

The detectives meticulously searched the area. Fortunately, they discovered an ATM camera near the crime scene and another camera on the house of the victim's neighbour.

With only five hours remaining before the potential attack, they immediately secured the footage and began reviewing the recordings. While examining the ATM footage, they identified the black van and captured the argument between Rashid and Vincent. Cross-referencing the traffic camera footage with the same timestamp, they tracked the van heading towards the vicinity of the crime scene. Roy also reviewed the traffic cam footage of Vincent and noted its proximity to where the van was seen. He surmised that their hideout must be located nearby.

"George, look," Roy pointed out, "they are heading towards our crime scene. I'm certain their hideout is close by."

"Yes, I agree. Have you reviewed the ATM footage yet?"

"No, not yet."

"Let's examine it quickly. I have a strong feeling we'll find something there," George urged.

Roy and George meticulously reviewed the ATM footage. Twenty minutes before Vincent's murder, they saw Vincent walking. Suddenly, he stopped, seemingly hearing a noise, and peered through the broken window of an old warehouse. Moments later, he ran down the alley.

"Yes! I believe we've found Rashid's hideout!" Roy exclaimed.

"Indeed, we have."

"Where is this place located?"

"It's an old warehouse, approximately two hundred meters from the crime scene."

"Call the FBI. We're going to raid that warehouse."

Roy contacted Richard and informed him of Rashid's suspected location.

"Richard, we've located Rashid's possible hideout. We're moving to raid it immediately."

"Send me the coordinates. I'll be there in a few minutes. Move swiftly; only two hours remain before the attack."

"Understood, we're on our way."

Immediately after the call, Roy and George, accompanied by the FBI team and SWAT, proceeded to raid the warehouse. Richard was en route via helicopter. The FBI surrounded the building. A team of ten heavily armed men, including Roy, approached the main entrance. Five more officers secured the rear of the warehouse to prevent any escape. Roads in the vicinity were also blocked. Once everyone was in position, SWAT breached the entrance and stormed inside. However, Roy was taken aback to find the warehouse completely empty. Richard and Mike arrived moments later.

"Man! This place is deserted," Richard exclaimed, his voice echoing in the empty space.

Roy then noticed a piece of furniture draped in cloth. Intrigued, he pulled back the covering and was stunned by what he saw.

Chapter 16: Countdown to the AVION MENACE.

T The planning board for the mission was a chaotic display of information: newspaper clippings, Pentagon blueprints, counterfeit Air Conditioner service contractor IDs, photographs of a private plane, its flight altitude, and the detonation time.

Roy and Richard stared at the board, a sense of urgency washing over them.

"Roy, I believe they've already initiated the mission," Richard said, pointing to the timing details. "It aligns perfectly with what Rashid told me earlier. The detonation is set for 5:00 PM, in exactly two hours. We must act swiftly."

"Look at these fake IDs for the Air Conditioner Service contractor," Roy added, his eyes scanning the board. "I'm guessing they plan to disguise themselves as repairmen."

Roy also noticed paint buckets and a photograph of a Johnson Air Conditioner Service contractor van.

"And this van photo," Roy continued. "They've likely painted a van to match the contractor's vehicle. That's how they'll gain entry."

"Roy, look at the circle drawn on the Pentagon's map," Richard exclaimed. "I believe that marks the balcony. No, wait! It's the terrace. They intend to detonate the E-BOMB on the terrace."

"Wait, what? What's an E-BOMB?" George asked, his voice filled with concern.

"It's an Electromagnetic Pulse weapon," Roy explained. "Its detonation will disable every electronic device within a 250-mile radius. This E-BOMB is incredibly powerful."

"Whoa, we need to move fast," George replied, his face paling.

"Mike, contact the Pentagon and inquire about the status of the air conditioning in Wing C," Richard instructed. "Ask if they've filed any complaints."

Mike made the call to the Pentagon office in Wing C, his expression turning grave as he received the information.

"The air conditioning has been out of service for two hours," Mike reported. "They've already contacted the air conditioner service contractor for repairs."

"Call Department of Defence Head Riley Maxwell," Richard ordered. "Tell them to lock down the Pentagon and initiate the EMERGENCY Code."

Mike relayed the threat to the Pentagon, and the Department of Defence immediately activated CODE 07, the emergency protocol for critical threats.

"Richard, notice the aircraft number written on the plane photo?" Richard said. "WD-3342. The altitude is also specified: 35,000 feet. I suspect they plan to detonate the E-BOMB in the air, just as Rashid described. And they've also noted the take-off location."

"Yes, it's a private airstrip seven miles from here," Roy confirmed.

Sofia, Max, and John arrived at the warehouse, having learned about the raid.

"Good, you're all here," Richard said. "We must move quickly. Roy and Sofia, you're heading to the airport. The FBI team will provide backup. Max and John, we're going to the Pentagon. Their security personnel are awaiting our arrival and will assist us in neutralizing the threat."

"Can I accompany you to the Pentagon?" George asked.

"Very well, you may," Richard conceded. "But refrain from taking any action unless instructed."

They swiftly departed for their respective destinations. Roy and Sofia, accompanied by FBI backup, sped towards the private airstrip, while Max, John, Richard, Mike, and George raced to the Pentagon.

Roy and Sofia, along with the FBI, arrived at the private airstrip in three vehicles. They immediately approached the airstrip and inquired about plane number 'WD-3342'. An official informed them that the passengers for that plane had arrived just ten minutes prior and were likely boarding. Roy and Sofia took the lead, searching for the aircraft. Soon, they spotted the plane and were shocked to see Bashir Hashemi, the leader of SCRIOS, boarding.

"Sofia! It's Bashir Hashemi," Roy exclaimed. "I believe he's leading the air mission."

"Yes, but how did he enter the States?" Sofia asked.

"The same way as Rashid, with a fake ID and passport. Let me get a closer look at all of them."

Roy used his smart lens to zoom in and observed Bashir carrying the E-BOMB onto the plane, accompanied by three other men: two pilots and a bodyguard. While Roy and Sofia were hiding behind some cargo, two of Bashir's security guards spotted them and aimed their weapons. The FBI team was unaware of Roy and Sofia's discovery, as they were searching for the plane in a different direction. The guards escorted Roy and Sofia to Bashir.

"Roy! You again," Bashir sneered. "You're a stubborn and lucky man, I must admit. After your narrow escape earlier, you should have sought safety. Now, you're going to die again. But don't worry, I won't simply shoot you. I have a more fitting plan for both of you."

"Bashir, whatever you do, you'll eventually meet your end," Roy retorted.

"Enough of your insolence, Roy," Bashir barked. "Guards! Take them onto the plane."

When the FBI arrived, they witnessed Roy and Sofia being forced onto the plane. The plane immediately took off, leaving them helpless. The FBI agents immediately contacted Richard, informing him of Roy and Sofia's abduction by Bashir Hashemi.

"Richard, Roy and Sofia have been abducted by Bashir Hashemi," the FBI agent reported.

"What! How?" Richard exclaimed.

"We were separated, searching for the aircraft in different directions. When we reached Roy and Sofia's location, we saw them being forced onto the plane at gunpoint," the agent explained.

"Damn! I hope they can do something. Should we shoot down the plane with one of our fighter jets?"

"But what about Roy and Sofia?"

"I know, but we can't risk the lives of thousands of innocent people for two individuals. Let me contact the Department of Defence for an immediate strike."

Richard contacted the Department of Defence, explaining the situation. They prepared to launch a jet to destroy the target.

"Richard, shouldn't we wait for Roy to contact us?" Mike asked.

"Don't worry," Richard reassured him. "The jet will take approximately thirty minutes for the operation. If we confirm Roy and Sofia's safety, we'll abort the mission. But it's better to be prepared than to regret it later."

Meanwhile, Max, John, Richard, Mike, and George arrived at the Pentagon. Richard and Max immediately met with Department of Defense Head Riley Maxwell, briefing him on the threat. Max, John, and George proceeded to the CCTV surveillance room.

"Immediately show me the parking area footage from the past hour," Max instructed. "Listen carefully, everyone. We're looking for a black van with the Johnson Air Conditioner Service branding."

The surveillance team began reviewing footage from various cameras. Given the Pentagon's vast size and numerous entry-exit points, locating the van proved time-consuming. After ten minutes, they spotted the van with the Johnson Air Conditioner Service branding. They tracked it to Wing C, where it was parked. Max dispatched a team to secure the van. Reviewing the garage footage, they saw Rashid, Abu, and an insider from the Pentagon helping them carry the E-BOMB inside the building.

Richard and Mike joined them in the control room to monitor the mission.

"Max, John, and George, you three must follow them immediately," Richard ordered. "Mike will track them through the footage and guide you via radio. Be cautious; he's armed and extremely dangerous."

"Understood, Richard," John replied. "Don't worry, we'll be fine. Let's go, Max and George."

The security head provided Max, John, and George with all-access passes. They immediately pursued Rashid and Abu. They encountered numerous security checkpoints, requiring them to swipe their cards to proceed.

"This security system is a nuisance," Max grumbled.

"Stay calm," George said. "We will stop the attack."

Mike guided Max, John, and George, directing them towards the location where Rashid and Abu, along with the insider, were planning to plant the E-BOMB.

After a few minutes, Mike reviewed the latest footage and saw Rashid, Abu, and the insider on the terrace, setting up the E-BOMB. Mike immediately informed Max, John, and George via radio.

"Rashid and Abu, along with another man, are on the terrace above Wing C," Mike reported. "They're setting up the E-BOMB. Proceed there immediately."

Max, John, and George raced towards the terrace. They soon confronted Rashid, Abu, and the insider. Mike identified the insider as a security staff member, planted by Bashir Hashemi.

Rashid, Abu, and the security guard saw Max, John, and George approaching with weapons drawn.

"They're coming for us, Rashid," Abu said.

"You two hold them off while I activate the E-BOMB," Rashid ordered.

Abu and the third man opened fire on Max, John, and George with advanced machine guns.

"Take cover! They're unleashing a hail of bullets," John shouted.

"How do we get out of this?" Max asked.

"I'll provide cover fire," George volunteered. "You two go and take them down."

"No, not you," Max protested.

But George ignored Max's plea and stood up, firing his weapon. To protect George, Max stepped in front of him and returned fire on Abu. However, George stumbled, his foot catching on a water pipe. Abu seized the opportunity and fired at George. Max instinctively dove in front of George, taking the bullet instead. He collapsed, unconscious. John immediately targeted Abu with his smart gun, killing him and the third man with a single shot.

John and George rushed to Max's side, seeking cover. Max clutched his stomach, where the bullet had struck. However, he found no wound. John then explained.

"Don't worry, you're not injured. We were sprayed with bulletproof liquid before the mission. It lasts for seven days, and today is the final day."

"Oh, thank goodness I'm alive," Max sighed in relief. "This spray is incredible."

"Thank you, Max, for saving my life," George said.

"You would have done the same for me," Max replied.

"Rashid is still there," John reminded them. "He's setting up the E-BOMB."

"Let's get that bastard," Max said.

Max, John, and George advanced towards Rashid. When Rashid saw them, he began firing while simultaneously working on the device. Max, John, and George returned fire. However, Max and John struggled to lock onto a target with their smart guns, making it difficult to shoot Rashid. In the final step of the process, Rashid needed both hands. As soon as he stopped firing and placed his hands on the controller, John stood up, locked onto the target, and fired, killing Rashid instantly. When John, Max, and George approached the E-BOMB, they were shocked.

"That bastard has already activated the E-BOMB," Max exclaimed. "It's set to detonate at 5:00 PM, with only 14 minutes and 20 seconds remaining."

Max informed Richard via radio, relaying the dire situation. Richard, accompanied by a cyber expert and a nuclear science expert, immediately rushed to the terrace and found the E-BOMB ticking.

Meanwhile, aboard the plane, Roy and Sofia were zip-tied and confined to a corner. Bashir initiated the activation process for the E-BOMB as the detonation time approached.

"I must thank your late father," Bashir said. "He was a genius, creating this small yet powerful device. No one else in history possessed the talent to create such a weapon."

"Bashir, you won't succeed," Roy said. "The FBI knows, and I'm sure they've already scrambled jets to destroy this airplane."

"Don't worry," Bashir said. "Even if they launch a missile, they won't be able to stop the E-BOMB. Once the timer is set, it cannot be stopped. The world will witness the power of SCRIOS. And don't worry, we won't die. See those suits? They're high-altitude suits with oxygen and parachutes. Once the timer is set, we'll jump out of the plane and land safely. So, best of luck to you both. You're going to die, either by a missile or by this E-BOMB. Guards! Take them to the other room and guard the door."

Roy struggled to free his hands. He suddenly remembered the laser feature on his watch, capable of cutting through anything.

"Sofia, help me activate the laser on my watch," Roy said. "We can use it to cut the zip ties."

"But how will we fight them? They have guns, and we don't," Sofia replied.

"Don't worry, we'll be fine," Roy said. "Remember, we were sprayed with bulletproof liquid. It lasts for seven days, and luckily, today is the last day."

"But what if the liquid doesn't work?" Sofia asked.

"We have to test it. Either way, we're going to die. Why not die trying?"

"Okay, come closer. Let me try to access your watch to turn on the laser."

Sofia helped Roy activate the laser. To their surprise, it worked, and they successfully broke free from the zip ties.

"Keep your hands behind your back. They mustn't know we're free," Roy instructed.

"Okay, what do we do now?" Sofia asked.

"Call that guard and ask him for water. As soon as he approaches, we'll attack him and take his gun."

"Excuse me, could I have some water? I'm not feeling well," Sofia said in a sweet and alluring voice.

The guard agreed and approached with a bottle. As soon as he opened the bottle, Sofia stood up and punched him hard. Roy wrapped his arm around the guard's neck from behind and strangled him.

Roy took the guard's gun, and he and Sofia left the room. From their hiding spot, they saw two other guards standing with Bashir. Roy instructed Sofia to scream, luring the guards to their location.

"AAAA, you bastard," Sofia screamed.

Bashir sent a guard to investigate.

"Go and see what happened," Bashir ordered.

As soon as the guard entered the room, Roy struck him on the forehead with the gun handle, causing him to faint. Sofia then strangled him.

"Where is that bastard? Why is he taking so long? Go and check on him. I'm about to finish activating this device. We'll be jumping out in five minutes," Bashir said.

The last guard entered the room. Like the previous guard, Roy struck him with the gun handle, and Sofia strangled him as soon as he fainted.

"Let's go," Roy said.

Roy and Sofia left the room and immediately prepared to confront Bashir. However, Bashir caught a glimpse of them and drew his weapon.

"Put it down, Bashir. Two against one are not favourable odds. You're going to die anyway."

"I don't care. I'll kill you both. You've ruined my plan. You'll both die, and this E-BOMB is already activated. Whatever happens, you're both going to die."

As Bashir aimed his gun at Sofia, preparing to shoot, Roy pulled the trigger and shot Bashir. Roy approached Bashir to confirm his death.

"Is he dead?" Sofia asked.

Roy sighed. "Yes, he's dead. But this bastard set the timer for only five minutes. We have four minutes and 11 seconds remaining."

"You go and handle the pilots, compelling them to land back at the private airstrip. I'll deal with the E-BOMB," Roy instructed.

"Okay. Look, this is a satellite phone. Call Richard immediately and seek his help to deactivate this E-BOMB."

"Right."

Roy dialled Richard's number and spoke with him.

"Richard, it's Roy. We're in the aircraft and have control over the E-BOMB. It's activated, and only three minutes and 52 seconds are left."

"Thank God you're both alright. I'll tell Mike to abort the fighter jet missile launch."

Mike immediately called and aborted the mission to destroy the aircraft with a missile.

"Our countdown is the same as yours," Richard said. "They've set the timer as planned. It's set to detonate at exactly 5:00 PM. We're trying desperately to deactivate it, but we're unable to."

"Damn! No problem, let me try," Roy said.

Roy began analyzing the E-BOMB, even pressing the red switch, but it didn't deactivate. Roy tried various methods, pressing buttons randomly in the hope of stopping it. But he failed, and time was running out.

"Richard, I can't deactivate it. Only 45 seconds left," Roy said.

"Get parachutes and jump out of the plane immediately," Richard urged.

"No, wait! Give the phone to Max."

"Max, there's a detachable circuit beneath the screen. On my count, remove it. I believe that will stop the E-BOMB."

"Hurry, only 10 seconds left," Max said.

"Okay, on my count: 3, 2, 1."

Roy and Max simultaneously removed the circuit, and the E-BOMB powered down.

"It's done, Roy," Max sighed in relief.

"Yes, it's done," Roy confirmed.

Roy then told Sofia, "Sofia, it's over. How far are we from the airport?"

"Thank God. We'll land in five minutes."

Roy and Sofia embraced with smiles. Richard, Max, John, and George cheered and hugged each other, relieved that the long and arduous day had come to an end.

Chapter 17: The Highest Honor.

Roy and Sofia disembarked the plane to find FBI vehicles awaiting them. They immediately boarded one and took custody of Bashir Hashemi's two pilots. With Roy carrying the deactivated E-BOMB and Sofia by his side, they returned to the Pentagon, escorted by FBI vehicles ensuring their safety and the security of the device. Within minutes, they arrived, and Richard greeted them warmly.

"Roy! Sofia! Well done, both of you!" Richard exclaimed, handing them chilled beers in celebration.

"Tell me, Roy, what sparked the idea about detaching that circuit?" Richard asked, taking a refreshing sip.

"Remember when I attached that circuit, and the machine powered on?" Roy explained. "I reasoned that detaching it would break the circuit signal and halt the process. Moreover, time was critical, so I had to take the chance."

"You know, you performed exceptionally well under immense pressure," Richard commended. "You are a truly valuable asset to this agency, Roy."

"Thank you, Richard," Roy replied, "but I must acknowledge my father's brilliance in designing this device and incorporating safety measures to prevent it from falling into the wrong hands."

"Indeed," Richard agreed. "Cheers to Roy and his ingenious father, Dr. Victor Spectre!"

"Cheers!" Roy echoed.

"Cheers!" the entire team shouted, raising their beers and savouring the cold sips with a collective sense of relief.

Roy addressed his team, "Thank you, everyone – Sofia, Max, John, Mike, and yes, George too. You all played crucial roles in this mission. Through our combined efforts, our country is now safe and even stronger. Cheers to the UNITED STATES OF AMERICA!"

The team erupted in cheers, clinking glasses in a heartfelt toast. Sometime later, Richard received a call from the President himself.

"Richard, you and your team have done a magnificent job. Congratulations, and thank you for safeguarding our nation. You will all be honoured with the Medal of Honor for your bravery. Please extend my personal thanks to Roy; he performed admirably."

"Thank you, Mr. President. I will certainly convey your message to Roy."

Richard hung up and turned to his team. "Guys, I just received a call from the President. He's incredibly pleased with our team's success, and we're all going to receive the Medal of Honor, including George!"

"Me too? That sounds fantastic!" George exclaimed, a wide smile spreading across his face.

"Wow! The Medal of Honor from the President! That's incredible, especially on our first mission. This is awesome, guys!" Max added, his voice filled with excitement.

"And Roy," Richard continued, "I almost forgot to mention, the President was particularly impressed with your performance and expressed his personal gratitude."

"Wow! That's amazing! I'm so happy today. Drinks are on me tonight at the best pub in town!" Roy declared.

Richard, Max, John, Sofia, George, and Mike all cheered in unison, "Yes!"

They celebrated late into the night. Finding a quiet moment, Sofia turned to Roy.

"Hey! Want to unwind a little more privately?" she asked, a playful glint in her eyes.

"Oh yeah, absolutely," Roy responded, his voice husky.

"Then follow me," Sofia said, taking his hand.

Roy and Sofia went to Sofia's apartment, their embrace deepening with each step. As they entered her room, their passionate kisses intensified. Sofia tore Roy's shirt open, and Roy gently removed Sofia's elegant dress, unclasping her bra. Their kisses trailed towards the bedroom. Sofia playfully pushed Roy onto the bed, removed his pants, and climbed on top of him. They shared a profound connection of love, passion, and emotion in a beautiful act of intimacy.

The next morning, they awoke in each other's arms.

"Last night was wonderful," Sofia murmured. "Could we do it again and again?"

"Oh, I would love that," Roy replied, his eyes filled with affection.

"What about right now?" Sofia suggested, her fingers tracing his chest.

"Again! I would love to. I adore these kinds of good morning wishes," Roy said with a smile.

They indulged in a second, energetic "good morning," savouring the rest of the day in each other's company.

Three days later, Mr. President summoned Richard, Roy, Sofia, Max, John, Mike, and George to the White House.

They arrived, a sense of pride swelling within them as they entered the iconic building, anticipating the honor they were about to receive. They gazed in awe at the White House corridors, absorbing its history, admiring its architecture, the art pieces and photographs adorning the walls, and the beautifully appointed rooms. It was a truly mesmerizing experience. Finally, they reached the magnificent and historic Oval Office, the President's chamber. The President greeted them warmly.

"Welcome, my heroes! Congratulations on successfully completing such a challenging mission and saving our beloved nation from a grave threat."

The President's aide then presented the Medals of Honor. Mr. President personally pinned the medals above each of their hearts and shook their hands. When he reached Roy, he said, "Excellent work, Roy. You are a tremendous asset to our nation. Your bravery and intelligence are truly commendable. I wish you all the best for the future."

"Thank you, Mr. President," Roy replied, his voice filled with gratitude.

And with that, another chapter in Roy's life drew to a close, promising endless adventures in the future alongside his exceptional team, driven by their unwavering dedication to safeguarding the nation from imminent dangers and neutralizing anyone who dared to threaten its security.

Acknowledgments

My sincere gratitude goes to my wife, Krishna Jariwala, for her unwavering support throughout the writing process of this book. Her steadfast confidence in me was instrumental in bringing this project to fruition.

I would also like to thank Vishnu Bagdawala for his invaluable assistance in locating resources that enriched the narrative and strengthened the book.

A special thank you is owed to my friend, Jatin Puri, whose insightful feedback and guidance were crucial in refining both the story and my writing style. His valuable advice played a significant role in making my first book a complete reality.

Author Notes

With the unveiling of "The Avion Menace," my debut novel, I embark on an exciting new chapter in my life as an author. This spy thriller took shape during the quietude of lockdown, born from a long-standing fascination with the intricate worlds of intelligence and espionage. Through meticulous research, I have strived to immerse the reader in a tapestry of adventure interwoven with threads of mystery.

In the character of Roy Spectre, I have sought to create a compelling protagonist—a unique blend of unwavering bravery, sharp intellect, and profound emotional intelligence. It is through this multifaceted character that I envision exploring a spectrum of thrilling adventures in my future literary endeavours.

Within these pages, each character, no matter the size of their role, holds a vital significance to the narrative. I have carefully crafted each portrait to ensure their contribution is both meaningful and substantial to the unfolding events.

The journey of writing this book has been a transformative experience, igniting my imagination and bolstering my confidence. It has been a profound lesson in unlocking the boundless creativity within, a process I fondly refer to as opening the doors to my personal "idea factory."

The experience of writing "The Avion Menace" has been immensely rewarding, and I have savoured every step of this journey towards publishing my first book. It is my sincere hope that you, the reader, have enjoyed the thrilling adventure of Roy Spectre.

For those interested in gaining insights into my writing process and exploring glimpses of my daily life, I invite you to connect with me on Facebook and Instagram.

Thank you once again for your invaluable support.

Sincerely,

Pranav Jariwala.

www.ingramcontent.com/pod-product-compliance
Ingram Content Group UK Ltd.
Pitfield, Milton Keynes, MK11 3LW, UK
UKHW041313190726
13845UKWH00025B/239

9 789354 087486